Party Girl
Author: Ewing, Lynne
Reading Level: 4.7
Point Value: 4.0
Quiz: 24911

An old bent woman biting a thick cigar gave me a strange look and walked over to the entrance, the hem of her long yellow dress sweeping across the floor.

"Ah, you a bad one, you are," she said, the cigar wagging at the corner of her mouth as she spoke. "You got no future. No future on your face. None at all." She smiled and blew smoke into my face.

I breathed in the acrid smoke.

"You need a cure, I think. I could give you what you need. But you got to pay the price, eh?"

She slammed the door.

I stood looking at my reflection, wondering what she had seen in my face. That I was a murderer? Had forced my best friend onto the street? I felt suddenly hot even with the devil winds spinning down the street.

D0048700

LYNNE EWING

Published by
Dell Laurel-Leaf
an imprint of
Random House Children's Books
a division of Random House, Inc.
1540 Broadway
New York, New York 10036

Text copyright © 1998 by Lynne Ewing
Cover art copyright © 1999 by Jeff Mangiat

Visit us on the Web! www.randomhouse.com/teens

Educators and librarians, for a variety of teaching tools, visit us at www.randomhouse.com/teachers

ISBN: 0-375-80210-X

RL: 6.5

Reprinted by arrangement with Alfred A. Knopf,
a division of Random House, Inc.

Printed in the United States of America

First Laurel-Leaf edition May 2001

20 19 18 17 16 15 14 13 12 11

OPM

for Marda and Jack Ewing

The light shines through the darkness,

and the darkness can never extinguish it.

—John 1:5

La luz en las tinieblas resplandece,

y las tinieblas no prevalecieron contra ella.

—S. Juan 1:5

PARTY GIRL

God is the dream maker, and I prayed to the Holy Mother of God to awaken me from this nightmare. Wind blew against the church like dangerous swirling floodwaters. I imagined the wind blowing the old mission church from its foundation and spinning Ana and me over the smogged Harbor Freeway across the Pacific Ocean and dropping us on some tropical land beneath purple orchids and yellow singing birds. I held Ana's cold arm as if to tell her to wait. Then I slipped my old fourth-grade picture from my jacket pocket. My front teeth looked too big for my mouth then, even with a smile so big that it curled my cheeks into my blue eyes until I looked like I was squinting at the sun. I pinched the picture and slid it down Ana's lacy blouse, slowly. My trembling fingers pushed the picture to where her heart lay, still as a stone inside her rib cage. I don't think anyone saw me. It was too dark. Power lines had fallen to the Santa Ana winds earlier that morning. So now flickering candles lit the sanctuary and made shadows appear behind everyone like shimmering ghosts.

It was a mistake to let myself get carried away with imagining the ghosts because a shudder rose from deep inside me, a pale moon of dread. I couldn't stop the chattering of my teeth. I have too much imagination. All my life I have seen things that weren't really there. Visions. Nightmares. That's why my friends call me Dreamer.

I don't know if it was the ghost shadows, the crying wind, or the cloyingly sweet smell of carnations that made me feel so dizzy. I grabbed the edge of Ana's white casket to steady myself and knocked over a pink teddy bear someone had placed on the pillow beside her. A stack of photos under the bear slid across the white satin with a slick sound that sliced into me. A Polaroid picture of Ana holding two guns stared up at me. I turned it facedown with a sharp slap. Ana hated guns.

I knew. We had been best friends since fourth grade—outcasts, both of us. I had been kept back a year because I had missed too much school taking care of my mother. Ana had come from Mexico with her parents and didn't speak

English yet. That was the year it took two of us to make one person. Ana and Kata. No one said one name without calling the other. I spoke for Ana even though I could barely speak for myself. I protected her. Later she helped me pass tests so I could stay in school.

We used to sit on the playground and plan our weddings, tracing long flowing white gowns in the sand with sticks. In our imaginations the lace trains swept across the edge of the playground, carried by little girls in white ruffled dresses. Then in sixth grade—I can't remember the day it happened—a stone rolled in front of our futures. We dropped the sticks and our dreams and started planning our funerals instead.

Ana wanted a blue dress and an ebony casket to carry her to eternity. Her mother and sisters laughed when she bought the blue dress. They told her she was crazy to buy a prom dress before she even had a date. They didn't understand that Ana was buying her shroud.

Now Ana lay in a white gown like a child taking first communion, a white prayer book pressed in her hands, the stiff lace scratching her for eternity. Maybe I should have told her mother about the blue dress that hung in her closet in a pink bag, but I knew she didn't need more to cry over. I was never going to tell her. About the dress. About Ana's secret life. How could I give her more sadness?

Ana was dead because of me. She didn't want to go to

the battle of the go-go's Tuesday night. She wanted to study for her algebra test. But those devil winds swept down from the desert that night, breathing against my bedroom window, calling me with their stormy voices and scraping the bony branches of the dead apple tree back and forth across my window, demanding that I run wild with them. I couldn't stay home with the wind calling me and my mother and her demon lover making love noises in the living room as if I weren't even in the house.

"Come on, the party scene is nothing without us," I whispered into the phone, trying to persuade Ana to come out with me.

When she didn't answer, I made my voice like the wind. "It's a big contest," I whispered. "You want to win, don't you? We got to keep our reputation. All that practicing, the blisters on our feet, that was for nothing?"

I knew I could talk her into it. Her home had become too small for her, with her perfect sisters and perfect mother crowding around her. Only the night was big enough to hold our wild spirits.

"The night belongs to us," she said finally. That was our code to meet at the corner of Arden and Fifty-third.

Ana had to sneak out of her house.

I didn't. Mom was passed out in front of the TV in her bikini panties and bra. Her boyfriend, some man I didn't know in his skivvies, a guitar resting on his knee, saluted me with two fingers as I grabbed my black trench coat and walked out the door. Mom was always bringing home men and introducing them to me as my new dad. When I was still too young to understand, she'd point to a man walking down the street and breathe into my ear, "There goes your daddy, baby. Go catch him."

I'd run after the stranger, hoping to find what other children had. That was how she used to pick up men. Now I ran down the street to meet Ana, my coat flying behind me like a witch's cape, my high heels tapping a staccato beat on the cracked cement sidewalk. The wind blew through my hair, tousling it around my head like a bed of kelp in a worried sea.

Ana was already at the bus stop.

"Dreamer!" Ana yelled when I turned the corner. She carried a black plastic purse filled with bottled water, bananas, and honeysuckle. She rolled her butt, the red go-go shorts tight on her rump, her legs long in the five-inch heels that matched mine. I opened my coat to show her my outfit, a mirror image of hers. We wore our white blouses low-cut and provocative over satin bras specially made for us at Trashy Lingerie.

An old woman with a fallen stomach, gripping plastic grocery bags in her swollen fists, looked at Ana, then at me.

"Desgraciadas," she said, and stepped away from the bus bench as if we had something contagious.

Ana and I laughed.

"Ah, it's okay, viejecita," Ana said. "You can't catch what we got. Nobody can. You got to be born with it."

"¿No tienen vergüenza?" she asked.

"Oye, we know what we're doing, revealing our bodies," I said. "I'd rather tease than please. No boy's going to own me the way my mother gets owned."

The bus pulled up to the curb with a hiss of air brakes. Ana and I waited for the woman to hobble on board. I tried to help her with the bags, but she pulled her hand away from me and made a spitting noise.

We followed her onto the crowded bus and dropped our coins in the meter, then ran to the back, looking for a place to sit as the bus pulled away from the curb, making everyone tilt wildly. I could feel the eyes of everyone on us. The men looked at us without moving their heads so their wives and girlfriends couldn't see them stare.

The women stared openly, some with cold eyes, hissing and calling us names under their breath. But others had a different look, as if their souls had left their bodies and gone with us. Those women needed to dance, and when they didn't, their souls went on to the dance without them, leaving them with just a husk of a body, as dry as bones, sitting alone on the bus. I pitied those women who had given everything for their families and kept nothing for themselves, not even a dance.

We fell giggling into the seat at the back of the bus, next to the woman with the grocery bags. A young mother with a baby turned and smiled at us. She looked about our age, her eyebrows as thin as knife cuts, her eyelashes spiked from layers of mascara. Ana stopped laughing and looked at the dark pressing against the bus window.

"Is Pocho going to be there?" I asked Ana.

"I didn't tell him," she said.

"He'll be mad," I said.

"Yeah? What right does he have to be angry? He doesn't own me." Her words tumbled out, an avalanche of sudden anger. "I hate the way everyone thinks I have to tell Pocho everything."

"You're his lady," I said.

"Did you tell Kikicho?" Ana said.

"Of course," I said.

"Then where is he?" Ana said.

"He couldn't come," I said.

"So Pocho's probably doing something, too," she said, and shrugged.

"But I invited Kikicho. You should have at least called Pocho."

"Forget it," she said, and looked out the window again. Something was bothering her big time.

We got off the bus in the old warehouse district near Fourth Street. It must have seemed strange to the people on board: two girls dressed for a party getting off at a vacant lot filled with discarded mattresses, rusted car frames, and shadows as black as midnight.

Ana's mood seemed light again.

"On the count of three," Ana said, "turn and see how many people on the bus are still looking at us. Okay?"

"I bet they all are," I said.

We counted, then turned on three. Everyone was staring out the bus window. Even the driver glanced back at us.

"Outrageous Chaos!" we yelled. I opened my coat, and Ana and I shimmied.

"No one's ever going to forget us," I said as the bus rolled away, snorting exhaust in our faces.

The old woman with the grocery bags smiled a toothless grin from the back window as if she thought God had rained the bus pollution on us.

The woman turned back, but not before raising two crooked fingers in a curse.

"Why'd she do that?" I said.

"Cada loca con su tema," Ana said, and shrugged. "Besides, we're not superstitious."

"A curse doesn't have anything to do with superstition," I said. "You pray, right?"

"That's different."

"A curse is just an upside-down prayer. Why'd she have to do it?" I felt nervous about the night now.

"Come on," Ana said, her voice loud and echoing into the night. "She can't hurt us, not that old woman. We're Outrageous Chaos, remember?"

I looked at Ana. Something was wrong. Her voice sounded desperately happy, like a person laughing when she really wanted to cry. She grabbed my hand and pulled me down the dark street, wind pushing our backs, toward the distant music.

The dance battle was held in a deserted warehouse. Crowds of young people lined the entrance, handing over money to two men wearing yellow sweatshirts.

We ran to a side entrance where security guards in yellow parkas huddled like football players trying to stop a touchdown. They stepped aside when they saw us. Some even remembered us from other competitions and said, "Hey, O.C."

Ana and I called our dance crew Outrageous Chaos, but the guys all called us O.C.

Inside, girls stood in clusters doing each other's hair, practicing steps, testing red and brown lipsticks, painting fingernails black, and smoking cigarettes. They eyed us when we entered, sizing us up. Ana and I acted cool, like the competition meant nothing, but already my heart was thumping. I took off my coat and stretched. I lifted my leg against a wall, rested my head on my knee, and counted to ten. I liked the feel of my legs, the muscles pulling bone, totally in my control. Ana slipped honeysuckle blossoms into my blond hair, weaving the stems into the wind-tossed tangles. Then she wove the flowers into her black hair, her fingers working quickly. When she was finished, she wore a crown of pale pink and white flowers that looked like a halo.

"I love you, Ana," I said. "You're the best friend I've ever had or ever will have."

"You're my best friend, too," she said, and kissed my forehead, then used her thumb to rub away the lipstick stain.

We were fifth to go on. Flashing red and blue lights swept over the crowd and stage. The room smelled of sweat, smoke, beer, and longing. Three, maybe four hundred people were there. Guys mostly, in bagged-out jeans and Pendletons and baseball caps worn backward, but some girls stood in the audience checking out the competition and trying to keep their boyfriends in line. When we walked onstage, guys clapped, whistled, and yelled, "O.C. O.C." It felt like everyone knew us. We worked hard to build a big reputation. We practiced until our muscles felt like rubber and our feet throbbed, and then we practiced some more. Anything felt possible if the music was right.

The pounding bass beat started, shaking the corrugated metal walls, making my heart beat louder, faster. Ana and I danced.

We began like boats on the waves, up and down, Ana

with her hands on my hips, our bodies working as one, swaying with the rhythm of the tides until we became the waves themselves moving across a distant ocean. Finally we were the music, floating free. This was better than any drug. We danced and the audience followed us in a trance, forgetting their problems and soaring into the night.

We kept moving, undulating, sweat dripping from our bodies. Our feet intertwined, a slow trickle of steps that rushed into a cascade of spinning footwork, without a stumble. Ana and Kata skipping over sea foam.

Honeysuckle blossoms dropped from our hair. Guys jumped onto the stage and scooped up the wilted flowers, then jumped from the stage and held the sweet flowers to their noses.

Some girls slapped their boyfriends for looking at us with such hot-blooded desire. Others took their boyfriends to the dark shadows in the back, kissing, blouses unbuttoned, jeans unzipped, hands seeking love but never finding it.

We knew the music had stopped when the guys started clapping and our souls fell back to earth. Ana smiled at me, and I smiled back. Dancing was our deliverance.

"Kata, you're the best," she yelled above the applause. "Your dancing has duende."

"Magic?" I yelled back. "I just follow you."

"No," she said. "You got it. The talent."

We floated off the stage, the clapping a roar of surf

behind us, and couldn't feel the blisters bleeding in our shoes.

After us the contest became scandalous. Crews started stripping, not naked, but taking off shirts and dancing in fuchsia silk bras or slinking from their tight black skirts and dancing in Day-Glo pink panties. They had to do more to beat us—show more skin as a way to win.

Ana and I won anyway.

The security guards helped us sneak out the back. Too many guys wanted to meet us, so we couldn't wait for a bus at the stop. We walked home, eating bananas and drinking water, Ana swinging our trophy, the Santa Ana winds whipping our honeysuckle-smelling hair into our eyes. I pulled my coat tight around me.

At the corner of Arden and Fifty-third we stopped under the amber glow of the street lamp. Overhead, palm fronds scraped softly against each other, back and forth, lulling us with their constant rhythm into feeling safe and alone. On Fifty-third Street it was dangerous to ever feel safe. Our neighborhood was a war zone, divided by hatred stronger than barbed-wire fences. Kids I hadn't played with in elementary school were now my friends, and kids I had traded lunches with were now my enemies because we lived in different neighborhoods. We fought over crumbling cement and potholed streets that didn't even belong to us.

"You want to go to the field?" I asked. The field was a

vacant lot down by the L.A. River where we kicked it with our homies and drank forties and tequila.

She shook her head but didn't move to go home. At first I thought the wind was making her eyes water, but then I knew something was wrong.

"What's up?" I said. "You've been weird since the bus."

She shook her head and stood there shivering. I took off my coat and gave it to her.

"I'm pregnant," she whispered.

I felt a pinch of anger.

"You let Pocho own you?" I said. I couldn't believe she had kept something that big a secret from me. Then I saw Ana's sad face and knew from her expression that I had let her down gacho by getting angry and not listening.

"I'm sorry," I said. "What do you want me to do?"

She didn't say anything. Her face, half in light, half in shadow, looked like a mask. She was frightening me the way she stared at me.

"Didn't you want to get pregnant?" I asked. In our neighborhood girls were happy when they got pregnant. Some even tried to get pregnant, putting holes in condoms or lying about taking the pill, so they could face out, quit the gang life, and collect their welfare. They sexed boys they didn't even like because they were dreaming so hard about babies. I thought about Pocho, how happy he was going to be.

"I wanted to get pregnant so I could get out of the life," she said, but her eyes drifted like she was talking to someone behind me. "It scares me, the things we do. Don't you think about it? The fighting? The partying? What are we going to do when we're viejas? Hang out at the river and show off our skinny-bone butts to the boys?"

I laughed. I couldn't imagine two old ladies doing what we did.

"But now I'm scared about this," Ana said.

"Don't think about the future," I said. "We're party girls, ésa."

"Yeah, don't think about the future, because we don't get one," she said.

Ana was only fourteen. Her mother and sisters were planning a big quinceañera for her. Her family didn't have much, but they celebrated everything. They loved Ana, and their love blinded them to seeing the life she lived. None of them saw the fear that gripped her heart every morning when she stepped out the front door. Every day she walked to school, eyes darting, scoping the neighborhood, wondering if this was the day she'd get blasted. Our school sits in the middle of enemy territory. No way around it. You want to go to school? You have to go through it. I had to go to school so Mom could get her welfare. Ana had to go to school because she loved the reading and the learning, even the math. I wasn't smart like Ana. Teachers said she'd go to college. The same teachers told me I'd end up in prison if I didn't die first.

"I can't stop thinking about it," Ana said. "The risks we took jacking all those cars."

"That was fun," I said. "You liked it."

"We could have hurt someone," she said.

"But we didn't," I said.

"What about when we were chased down by the cops?"

"We got away," I said. "And now it's a funny story to tell our homies."

"But it still makes my heart race. Sometimes I lie in bed and think of what we did, and then I pray to Mother Mary to look into her heart and pray for me."

"You were never scared of anything," I said. "Not even hell."

"Don't tell me you believed my act." Ana laughed bitterly. "Cuidado, or you'll start to believe your own."

I searched her face, trying to see her fear.

"I was always scared," she said. "And now I'm scared of this. How am I going to tell my mom?"

Ana brushed the hair from her face. Her eyes met mine, and for a moment I saw another person inside Ana's body, someone trapped and wanting to break free. She turned from me and faced the wind, but I had already seen tears edge to the corners of her eyes.

"Your mom loves you," I said, wishing I had been born to

Ana's mother. "Just tell her. What's the problem? Lots of girls at our school are pregnant or have kids."

"My sisters got married first," Ana said. "And what about Amelia?"

Amelia was her younger sister, behind us two years in school. Ana was always fussing over her and telling her what to do so she wouldn't get in trouble.

"I don't want Amelia to fall into the life," she said.

"Don't worry. Amelia can take care of herself. Your mom's going to understand, and Pocho's going to be really happy," I said.

"It's not Pocho's," she said, and passed her hands over her face as if she were pushing away a sad memory. "Pocho and I haven't. I don't love him."

The wind was playing tricks with me, stealing words from Ana's mouth. She couldn't have said Pocho wasn't the father, but already my mind was going through all the guys in the gang that she might have been with. I couldn't think of any. Pocho wouldn't let any of the guys hang around her. He was too jealous.

"What's Pocho going to do when he finds out?" she said.

"He'll understand," I said, but that wasn't what I was thinking. Pocho thought he was the baddest cholo in L.A. County. He was paranoid and jumpy. Even if someone bumped into him accidentally, he acted aggressive and out of control. Some girls thought that made him more of a man, but I knew Pocho's real story. He hated me for knowing the soft places inside him. There was always a tension between Pocho and me, as if someday we were going to have to fight it out. Maybe it was going to be over this. Ana's baby.

"We could run away," I said. I'd been begging Ana to run away for a long time. "You and me, we could raise the baby. I could get a job, lie about my age, pick up money dancing in bars or steal it from some gabachos."

She shook her head. "There's no escape."

Then in the distance tires squealed. A motor revved, and a Chevrolet Monte Carlo blasted out of the darkness and turned the corner, its headlights blinding me.

"You recognize it?" I asked.

The car slowed, then stopped in front of us.

"Who is it?" Ana asked. "Can you see?"

I didn't recognize anyone. The guys all had the look, but they didn't have the dead eyes of guys on a mission. Lots of times after the go-go battles, guys tried to find us, flirt with us, and ask us out.

"Just a bunch of busters," I said.

"Nobodies," Ana said, but the sound of her voice made me think she was mocking me.

The back window rolled down, and a sawed-off shotgun pointed at us from the backseat. The shadowy face over the gun yelled an enemy gang name in a low, growling voice.

I jumped behind a Dodge parked near the street corner and rested my face in the wet grass, waiting for them to blast us.

"You down, Ana?" I said, the grass flicking my tongue and lips as I spoke, the taste of dirt filling my mouth.

When Ana didn't answer, I looked up. She stood at the corner, waiting for bullets. At first I thought she was showing how brave she was. That's how she got her street name, Chancey: always taking chances. I thought she'd duck at the last second.

Instead she faced the car defiantly, throwing our gang sign, my black coat flapping behind her like giant wings.

"Ana!" I screamed.

The guy holding the gun hesitated as if he didn't know if he should shoot a girl or not, or maybe he was seeing Ana's face, her soft, beautiful angel eyes, and he was falling in love with those eyes that were right now daring him to kill her.

"Ana, get down!"

"I chose the music," Ana said. "Now I'm going to dance."

I sprang from behind the Dodge as angry white fire split the night. Ana and I rolled to the ground with gunfire spraying over us, hitting trees, chipping the cement curb, and shattering car windows.

The Monte Carlo screeched away, turning the corner too tight. The hubcaps scraped against the curb, showering red sparks onto the sidewalk.

I clung to Ana, the smell of honeysuckle filling my lungs, my ears still ringing from the gunshots.

"Chancey, you're as crazy as it gets. Wait till I tell everyone what you did."

Ana didn't answer.

Then I felt something warm and frightening soak into my blouse and trickle across my chest and neck, finally mixing with my tears.

A siren rose above the wind's wailing, and footsteps gathered on the sidewalk, crunching dead leaves and gravel, stopping a respectful distance from where I lay with Ana on top of me. In the dark sky overhead a helicopter's blades thumped. Then a white spotlight shone down on us. A sheriff's car pulled to the curb, and red and blue flashing lights slid over us for the second time that night.

Finally paramedics lifted Ana off me, placed her on a stretcher, and carried her to the back of an ambulance, her blood dripping on the grass, the street, the ambulance floor.

I stood. Ana's blood covered my blouse. Tiny rivulets streamed down my arms and legs. People thought I had been shot, too.

An old woman with deep wrinkles in her leather face crossed herself and said, "Milagro."

Then another woman, her black shawl flapping wildly around her face, said something about the devil winds bringing me back to life, and they all stepped away from me as if the wind had possessed my body.

A paramedic sat me on the ground and wrapped a blanket around my shoulders.

"I'm not hit," I said. "It's Ana. Get her to the hospital."

He smiled at me sadly. "Just let me check you," he said.

"It's Ana's blood," I said. "Not mine. Please, take her to the hospital. Don't waste time on me."

He took my blood pressure anyway and checked my arms and legs and chest. Then he snapped his red case closed and stood and stared at the long black tire marks on the street as if he were trying to decide where to go.

"It could have been you, you know?" he said. His voice sounded sad. I didn't know who he was talking to at first. "Maybe you should think about how this would have hurt your parents—if you had been the dead girl."

That was when I knew Ana got out for good. Rest in peace.

He looked back at me as if he couldn't go until I gave him an answer.

I drew in a deep breath to steady my voice.

"The only one who cared just died," I said softly.

"Sorry," he said. Then he turned and walked toward the fire department truck as a deputy sheriff walked over to me, her uniform tight over her hips and belly, her heavy shoes scraping against the sidewalk.

The deputy gave me her card. She wanted to know my

name and address and the name of the gang I belonged to. I stared at her. I didn't have a name without Ana to call it. It had taken the two of us to make one for so long that I wasn't sure I existed without Ana. My hands started shaking.

I began to weep, and the deputy sat down beside me. She crossed her legs and didn't seem to notice the ocean of blood around us.

"You know who did it?" she asked. "Is that why you're scared? That they'll come back and get you? I can help you if you help me."

"I didn't see anything," I said. I shook my head and pushed the tears away from my eyes.

"What gang did your friend belong to?"

"She was a good student," I said. "She wasn't mixed up with anything. Tell her mom that. It was my fault. I'm the banger. Ana was a good kid. We just danced together. That's all."

She put her hand on my shoulder. Her skin smelled of Ivory soap and gun oil and a good life. "I know better than that," she said softly.

"Just tell her mother," I said.

"Call me if those punks come back and give you any trouble," she said.

"I'm okay," I said.

She looked at me like she didn't believe me. "Keep the

card in a safe place," she said, and stood, her leather belt and shoes cracking from the movement.

I pitched the card into the pool of blood. The last thing I needed was for anyone to think I had turned rata and was helping some deputy sheriff. I'd never disgrace myself by testifying, even against a rival gang. I'd take death or prison first.

"Look, I know you kids don't like the way the law works," she said. "You think the only justice is revenge. But the fighting's never going to stop if you don't stop the retaliations."

"I don't know what you're talking about," I said, even though I was already planning how to avenge Ana's death.

"I know you do," she said, and handed me another card. "You call me any time, day or night. You think about what I said. Your friend's dead, and now you have to make a choice. Don't lie to me and say you don't. It's your choice."

"I don't got choices in this neighborhood," I said. "If I had choices, you think I'd stay here?"

I watched her walk back to the sheriff's car and talk to her partner, the blue and red lights strobing over their faces.

She came back to me. "Come on, honey. We'll drive you home."

I sat in the back of the sheriff's car, shivering in spite of the paramedic's blanket still wrapped around my shoulders. I wished I had had the courage to tell Ana the truth, to tell her how I wanted out, too, to be just a normal kid, drawing wedding gowns on the playground with a stick. Maybe if she had known I was scared, too . . .

I held myself tight, the blood tacky on my skin. I couldn't stand that Ana was gone. The deputy was right. I wanted revenge. I wanted to kill someone for doing this to her. No one hurt Ana without payback from me. Those bangers were dead already. Muertos.

The sheriff's car rolled to a stop in front of my house. The deputy walked with me up to the front door, kicking through the yellowed newspapers scattered on the walk.

"I'll talk to your folks," she said.

I opened the door. Mom was standing in front of the TV in the middle of the living room, holding a cigarette in one hand, a beer in the other, singing some song I didn't recognize, maybe one her new stoner gabacho boyfriend had written. He was strumming his guitar, still in his skivvies, his eyes red from the cigarette smoke and beer.

When Mom finally saw me, the song stopped in her throat and the beer dropped to the floor, suds puddling on my grandmother's rug.

The deputy looked at Mom, then at me. "Sorry, kid. Don't forget to call me." She shook her head, turned, and walked away, her shoes hitting the sidewalk in rapid beats as if she couldn't get away from the sight of my mother's nakedness fast enough.

I ran to the bathroom and locked the door. I tore off my clothes and turned on the shower. I could hear my mother screaming at the man to get out. The front door slammed shut as I climbed into the steaming water. I let the fiery water pound my skin, my mother at the bathroom door, speaking through the keyhole.

"Kata. Kata! What happened, Kata?"

I hated the fine tremor that had crept into her voice. When the water turned cold, I turned off the spigot and stood in the steam.

I didn't know what to do without Ana. I didn't want to be here in this life without Ana.

I took a razor from the medicine cabinet, held it between my index finger and thumb, then slowly cut my skin, pressing hard, etching Ana's name into the web between my thumb and index finger, my blood dripping onto the white towel.

My mother remained at the keyhole, sobbing and calling my name, her breath rushing through the small hole, joining the wind shrieking around the house.

"I promise, baby," she said. "I promise I'll stop drinking. I'll be a mother again. I promise. Just say something. Talk to me."

She had made that promise too many times for me to believe her.

"Kata, baby, what happened?"

I never answered her.

That was the night Ana died.

With images from our last night together churning in my head, I leaned over and kissed Ana one final time, her red lips waxy and stiff. Then I walked away from the casket, past the old women crowded in the front pew, pinching off the beads on their rosaries, their heavy perfumes spinning in the air like a potion against death and evil, covering the musty smells of incense, prayer books, and ancient adobe walls.

Most of my homies sat in the back pew in shadows. They wore black sweatshirts with white Old English lettering across the front that said REST IN PEACE, CHANCEY. Kikicho had given me one to wear, but I couldn't wear it yet. I didn't want Ana's mother to know I was ganged up.

Maggie, fair-skinned with red hair and no cholo mix in her Anglo blood, had been in the gang since she was eleven. She had a sense of invincibility that made her seem like a good-luck charm. She passed out black satin ribbons for people to pin to their clothing. I had made photocopies of poems that Ana had written, but I felt too sad to hand them out, so Maggie was doing that, too.

I didn't want to sit with my homies. I did at all the other funerals, but this time I felt too angry to be with them. I knew they would say it was scandalous, the way I was acting, but I couldn't help it. I didn't like the way they acted, like Ana belonged to them. They didn't know her, really. A thought crept across my mind, whispering with cold, hateful breath that I hadn't known her either, not the way I thought. I raked my fingers through my hair to push the thought away, then paused at the edge of the altar, looking for a place to sit.

Kikicho stood on his metal canes and walked to the casket, his right leg dragging on the adobe floor. He balanced his canes against the coffin. The metal made a hard, clanking sound against the brass handles. Kikicho had three bullets inside him, one almost visible in his temple, one near his ear, and another somewhere in his back. Three other bullets had gone through his right leg. The doctors said he'd spend his life in a wheelchair.

I met him when he was in the wheelchair, making jokes about the bullets and pretending to stick a magnet to his temple. The magnet had drawn me to him. I took it from him and slipped it in my pocket. I didn't know him very well then, only that he was an old vato loco and I respected him too much to let him become Pocho's jester. He had paid his dues. Kikicho had something inside him, a softness of soul that made him handsome to me even though the other girls couldn't see his beauty. They wanted guys like Pocho who ran fast and hit hard and treated them badly.

"Come on," Kikicho said, and motioned with his chin for me to stand near the casket. He drew a camera from his pocket.

Pocho and Serena had already found places near the head of the coffin. Serena put her arm around Pocho and leaned into his chest, her face sad, her hands curled in our gang sign.

"Dreamer, oye," Pocho said. His hair and eyes were black as raven wings, but his face was as fair as the first conquistador to land in the New World.

"Come on, Kata," Serena said, waving me toward them with her perfect hands, the nails and rings glittering in the candlelight.

I shook my head.

"You guys were too mean to Ana," I said, "to take a picture with her now. It's scandalous."

They looked at one another as if each expected the other to understand what I was saying.

"You know what I'm talking about," I said. I stepped closer to the casket so the other mourners couldn't hear me. "Two years ago, what you did to her when we got jumped into the gang."

Ana and I were jumped into the gang the same day. Sometimes it's just girls jumping girls, but sometimes, if you want to join a gang with guys, too, then both hit on you. Ana went first. She was small, but she had lots of heart.

They pulled her hair and slapped her face and kicked her hard. That should have been enough, but then Serena ripped the gold hoop earrings from Ana's ears. Dark red blood curled down Ana's throat. She had to wear Band-Aids on her ears for two weeks and lie to her mother, saying the earrings got torn from her ears in P.E. during a basketball game. Her mother called the school, but no one from the school called back, so Ana was safe in her lie.

When they jumped me, I fought back so hard I broke Serena's nose. They were afraid to keep hitting me. I hadn't planned on hurting anyone. I was going to take my beating, show them I was down for the neighborhood. But Ana was holding a sweatshirt to her ears to stop the bleeding, and I couldn't let it go. Ever since we were niñas, I had defended her. No one hurt Ana and got away with it.

"Forget the earrings," Serena said now. "That was in the past. I was down for Chancey. We were best friends, her and me."

"No you weren't," I said, feeling the devil stir the anger bubbling up inside me.

Serena looked up at Pocho and pushed her fingers through her long brown hair. That's when I saw Ana's gold hoop earrings hanging in her ears.

"You take those off," I said to her. "I can't even believe you'd wear those earrings today and disgrace Ana's memory."

"Kata, stop," Kikicho said, and motioned for me to get

in the picture. "She's doing it to pay respect, to show her love."

Kikicho was always trying to make peace. I ignored him.

"You're disrespecting Ana," I said to Serena. "Put the earrings in the casket."

"Not today," Kikicho said softly. "Don't fight today."

"Take them off," Pocho said.

Serena shrugged and took off the earrings and slipped them under Ana's pillow. I looked away as Pocho and Serena held their hands in our gang sign and the camera flashed.

I stepped into a small alcove near the altar and stared at the gentle statue of our Lord Jesucristo that stood behind a line of candles. How many funerals had I been to? How could He allow another death?

A sudden gust of wind sent a draft through the sanctuary, making the candles flicker like wild tongues. My head felt thick. The statue shimmered and took a step forward, the alabaster hands reaching for me, a huge weight falling on me. I cried out and tried to run, but my feet refused to flee, becoming impossibly heavy, sinking into the adobe floor.

Then I felt soft hands wrapping around me.

"Jesucristo," I sighed, but those alabaster hands weren't the hands holding me. Ana's mother grabbed me before I fell and walked me back to her pew. She wore a black dress, her ankles swollen from the tightness of her patent-leather shoes. Ana's mother smelled of lilac powder, Aqua Net hair spray, and comfort. I wondered if she knew she was burying her grandchild along with her daughter. Had the deputy told her about Ana's secret life? Had the mortician shown her the gang name tattooed across Ana's belly in Old English letters?

Ana's mother looked down at me, her brown eyes red from crying. "Are you all right, Kata? Do you need some water?"

"I'm okay," I whispered.

She motioned to her daughters to make room for me on the pew, and we sat down together.

Then she saw where I had cut Ana's name on the web between my thumb and index finger. Scabs still covered the letters. She gripped my hand, her fingers as cold as Ana's. She drew my hand to her lips and kissed the scab of Ana's name. Her tears fell, warm drops on my skin between her cold fingers. The sudden change in temperature sent a chill over me. She wrapped her arm around me, pulling me to her, rocking us back and forth.

Ana's two older sisters, Margarita and Rosa, craned their necks around to look at me, their mascara running in black strings down their cheeks and necks, staining the tops of the white collars on their black dresses. I felt the glare of their hateful eyes staring at me. They gave me mean looks, as if I didn't belong there, sitting in the pew next to them with their perfect lives and working husbands and gold wedding bands.

Amelia poked her head from behind Margarita, her green eyes red and swollen with the loss of Ana. She flashed my gang sign at me. I pulled away, stepped over Margarita's and Rosa's knees, and squeezed into the pew on the other side of Amelia.

"Don't disrespect your mother or my gang," I whispered into her ear, the smell of her strawberry shampoo filling my nose. "You haven't been courted into the neighborhood, and I'm not going to let you in. That's my promise to Ana. You're not getting in. I won't let it happen."

Amelia turned away from me and stared ahead, anger and determination rising in her face. I had seen that look before. Amelia was hungry for the never-think-just-do life she thought we lived down by the L.A. River. When I was her age, it seemed exciting and romantic to me, too. Hanging out, listening to music played on a boom box, sloshing down forties, and not worrying about school or rules.

I stood and started back to my place next to Ana's mother.

"Make sure Kata gets Ana's bracelets and books," her mother said.

"How can you think about such things today?" Rosa said angrily.

"So she doesn't have to think about what you're thinking about," I said to Rosa.

Rosa shrugged. I could tell she was afraid of me.

"It's okay," I said, and sat back next to Ana's mother.

If I hadn't seen my grandmother at my grandfather's funeral, I would have thought Ana's mother didn't care, the way she was thinking about bracelets and books at her daughter's funeral. Death makes people say odd things as if nothing has happened. I think it's the only way they can get through what's going on.

The priest began talking, and his words carried me to memories of my grandfather. He had liked to go out to sea on a boat he had built himself. Fishing one day the boom came loose. It swept back and forth out of control and knocked him overboard. Three days later a family walking along the beach found what was left of him in a pile of kelp washed ashore.

Grandpa was a mamo, a shaman, a curandero with big magic. The first time he saw my grandmother, he was crossing an ancient suspension bridge high above the roiling Apurímac River near Cuzco in Perú. Her face appeared in the rising mists, and he knew he had to travel north to find her. Each night as my grandfather journeyed toward the United States, he and my grandmother met in his dreams. Somehow he knew he'd find her in Los Angeles, the city of angels. My name, Katarina Phajkausay, came from them both. Phajkausay means "peace" in Quechua, the language my grandfather spoke as a child. Katarina was my grandmother's first name.

After my grandfather's funeral my grandmother made his favorite fried chicken, marinated in lime juice and diced jalapeños. Everyone wondered how she could cook. I sat in the kitchen, hidden on a stool beside the broom closet, watching my grandmother's tears fall on the marinated chicken as she dipped it in flour and placed it in the crackling grease. Everyone said that chicken was my grandmother's best.

Now I imagined my grandfather with Ana in his boat, sailing across the universe.

"Take her to heaven, Machula," I whispered. "She don't belong in hell."

The priest stopped speaking, and people began whispering rapidly behind me with the soft chatter of sparrows after a storm.

Ana's uncles lifted the casket and carried it outside to the hearse.

I walked slowly behind.

My grandmother always said that God gives us suffering to mold us into the person He wants us to become, and as I stepped from the dim candlelit church into the whirling wind and blinding white light of day, I surely felt as if I were being kneaded by some powerful hand.

Wind littered the cemetery with eucalyptus leaves and broken branches. I waited away from the others in the old section, lost in a field of granite headstones and marble angels.

My homies stood, uninvited, at Ana's open grave. The security guard with the yellow beard had asked them to leave. When they wouldn't, he asked Ana's mother if she wanted him to call the sheriff. She didn't want the sheriff at Ana's funeral.

It had to be confusing to Ana's mother and sisters, sitting so rigid on folding chairs under the green plastic awning, wondering why these gangbangers had come to Ana's funeral. I prayed no one told them the truth: that we were Ana's other family.

A sudden gust of wind whipped the ribbons from Maggie's hand, and black satin strips fluttered around the mourners like dancing snakes.

My homies pushed around the casket, dropping pink and purple flowers onto the white lacquered surface as the machinery cranked and lowered Ana into the grave. Suddenly I saw us all lined up, pushing and crowding, trying to be the next one to climb into the casket with Ana. We were zombies, the walking dead, and maybe that was how we could do the things we did. Some part of us knew we were dead already. I hadn't shot anyone—yet—but I knew I could. Kill. I wanted to find the guy who killed Ana and blast him.

When I started to leave, a gentle breeze touched the

back of my neck and made me look up. I don't know what I expected to see. Machula with Ana in his boat, sailing across the clouds? I watched for a long time. Somehow I knew that Ana wasn't in the grave anymore, and I thought if I looked hard enough I might see her in the sky.

That afternoon we gathered down at the riverbed. I put on my black sweatshirt then and sat on a block of crumbling cement that had once been part of a flood-control channel. I didn't want to be there with everyone drinking and getting stoned, but Kikicho had talked me into coming because it was supposed to be for Ana. Kikicho sat next to me, his canes resting on the black mud and grass in front of us. I liked the way he stroked my back, soft and gentle, as if I were delicate and might break.

Pocho had stolen a white curly-haired puppy with brown spots like freckles across its face, and a long fuzzy tail. He yelled at the little dog, making it cower, tail between its legs, its fat belly shivering. Pocho laughed like it was really funny to see the puppy cringe. He was showing off for Serena. She was a fool to be impressed, but she was laughing like she was seeing a circus of clowns, her red lips waiting for Pocho's kiss now that Ana was gone. She had taken off her sweatshirt and unbuttoned her shirt, saying it was too hot, but we all knew what she was doing.

"Stop it, Pocho!" I yelled finally. "Leave the little dog alone."

"Don't watch him," Kikicho whispered, his breath warm and soft on my cheek.

"Don't tell me what to do," I said.

"I'm not telling you," he said, and took my hand.

"It sounded like it," I said.

"I just don't want Pocho to get you more upset," he said. "You don't need it today."

"I'm sorry," I said after a pause.

"¿Por qué siempre estamos peleando?" he said softly, and kissed my hand. "¿Qué problema hay?"

"We're not always fighting," I said, and then I smiled big and sweet the way my mother does at men to melt their anger.

Kikicho smiled back at me. "Come on, I'll make you that teardrop for Ana."

"Okay," I said.

He drew a tear under my right eye with an ink pen, then took a needle and began sticking it into my skin where he had drawn the teardrop to make a tattoo.

"You think she's close enough to see?" I asked. "Ana, I mean."

"Yeah," he said. "Yeah, I do."

I kept my eyes open the whole time, watching my reflection in the black pupils of his deep brown eyes as he pricked my skin with the needle. When he finished, he kissed the teardrop. A smear of blood and ink stained his full lips.

Then he kissed me so gently I wasn't sure our lips had touched until he kissed me again. He wasn't rough like other boys. Sometimes I wondered how he could like me when there were so many girls who did themselves up so fine to please the boys and let the boys own them, always ready to spread themselves.

"Why don't you get yourself a real girlfriend?" I said.

"You're my lady," he said.

"I don't give you what you want," I answered.

"How do you know what I want?" he said.

"I know," I said.

He shook his head.

"What?" I said.

"It feels like you want to start an argument with me."

"No, I don't," I said, but my words came out angry, and I knew he was right.

Then a squeal made me jump up. The puppy had started to pee, and Pocho, impatient to hold it, had yanked the dog into his arms before it had finished, and the dog had dribbled on his Pendleton. He cursed the dog and threw it down. The dog whimpered as if it understood the words. Pocho threw his beer can. Beer foam exploded over the dog and made it yelp and turn in tight circles.

Kikicho held my arm. He knew what I was thinking. I jerked away and ran to the shivering dog. I picked it up, kissing its ear, and wiped its wet fur with my sweatshirt.

"Pocho, you're a fool," I said. "Dogs don't give anything but love, and you treat it like this?"

"You don't even know what love is," Pocho said.

I wrapped the puppy in my sweatshirt and started walking away with it.

"Where you going?" Pocho yelled. "That's my dog." When I didn't stop, he ran after me and grabbed my arm, his black eyes dangerous and angry.

I pulled away from him. He grabbed my arm again and looked at me with hard, dull eyes.

"The others may be afraid of you, but not me," I said.

He tried to take the dog, but I wouldn't let him. "I *know* you, Pocho," I said in a fierce whisper through my teeth. I could hear Kikicho's canes rattling and thumping the soft ground, coming closer. Pocho's grabbing me was an insult too close to the bone. To save face, Kikicho had to fight him, but I knew he couldn't, not standing with two canes.

"The little dog doesn't want you anymore," I said, making each word slow and deliberate. I knew how to hurt Pocho. "Doesn't want you no more."

He pushed me away, and I started running, the puppy bobbing in my arms.

"Kata, come back!" Kikicho yelled.

"I got to get home to my mother," I said without looking back as I ran up the slope toward the freeway.

"Don't go by yourself," he yelled. "The guys that got Ana are probably out looking for you."

"I'll be careful," I said.

"It's not safe," he yelled back, anger breaking his words.

I was disgracing him by not going back, but I couldn't stand being there with all of them, drinking and smoking, the music pounding loud on the boom box and Ana in her grave.

When I reached the top of the slope, I turned back and stepped onto a cement wall that had once been used to guide floodwaters. "How can all of you act like this is a normal afternoon?" I shouted down at them. "Ana's not coming back."

Pocho grabbed Serena's malt liquor and threw it at me.

"We all loved Ana, you bitch," he yelled.

"Then why are you flirting with Serena like a matador courting a bull?" I said, and turned away.

The sun fell behind eucalyptus trees, pines, and oleanders, once a freeway beautification project to hide the flood-control channels, now a home to winos and the homeless. I hadn't gone far when I heard leaves crackling behind me.

I stopped and listened.

"Who's there?" I said softly, thinking Pocho might have followed me.

The wind rushed through the oleander branches, blowing the pink blossoms forward as if someone were making a path through the thick foliage toward me, but I couldn't see anyone in the moving shadows. Maybe it had only been the wind, or a cat, or someone's dog that had startled me.

I started walking again, the puppy whimpering in my arms, the wind howling around me, blowing dust into my eyes. That's when I heard someone's footsteps heavy behind me, like the hounds of hell padding after me to take me back where I belonged.

"Who's there?" I shouted.

When no one answered, I took off in a dead run, the puppy bumping against me. Whoever it was raced behind me, twigs breaking underfoot.

I turned toward the freeway underpass. A fire burned across my chest as I ran through the urine-soaked cement walkway and jumped across two homeless men lolling against the wall with a bottle of tequila.

Footsteps slapped behind me.

I burst out into an open field on the other side of the freeway, set the puppy down, and felt on the ground until my hands found a big rock. I hid behind a bottlebrush tree, my back tense and rigid, my hand ready to throw the rock.

Fear surged through my body, suffocating me with the certainty that there was someone near, watching me.

I waited a long time.

But nothing stirred. Had I only imagined the footsteps? I decided the only way to find out if someone was stalking me was to make myself visible. I held my breath and stepped from behind the bottlebrush tree.

"Come out and fight!" I yelled.

A breeze ruffled through my hair like a stranger's fingers. If someone was still there, hidden behind the oleander bushes, he chose not to show himself.

Finally I picked up the dog and walked to the street. I kept casting glances over my shoulder, expecting to see someone suddenly spring from a bush and grab me.

I stopped at Thrifty and went to the rows of vitamins in the back near the pharmacy. I wanted something for Mom, something to help her keep her promise, but I didn't know what to get her. When no one was looking, I stuffed brown bottles of vitamins C and A and multiples in the back pockets of my bagged-out jeans and pulled my sweatshirt low to cover the bulges. Usually Ana came with me, and I stole perfume and makeup while she kept the salesclerk busy with talk about condoms, tampons, and douches. Then on the way home we'd laugh at all the questions Ana had asked and try to think of new questions that were even more embarrassing for her to ask the next time. A rush of loneliness for Ana came over me. I held the puppy to my face, its wet tongue licking my nose, to keep the tears from coming. I wondered who could make me laugh again.

I grabbed a can of dog food, stuffed it in my waistband, and walked up to the cash register, my face a stone, the vitamins rattling in my pockets. I picked up a pack of Tic Tacs and shook them like maracas to cover the sound of the pills clicking in the bottles in my pockets. Then I gave the cashier a dollar.

The cashier didn't look at my face. Her eyes wandered through the store over boxes of chocolate-covered cherries and cans of tuna as if she were taking inventory.

I stopped shaking the Tic Tacs and tried to figure out what she was seeing. Then the store manager walked over to us with quick steps that made me nervous. My legs tensed, ready to dodge him and run out the door.

"Dogs aren't allowed in the store," he said, his voice like tumbling gravel.

"What?" the cashier said. She looked around her counter as if she were trying to find the dog, then looked up and saw the puppy resting in my arms.

"Sorry," I said, and shook the Tic Tacs. "I'll leave the dog home next time."

When the manager walked away, the cashier handed me the change. I took the coins, and when she looked away again I grabbed three rolls of Life Savers and walked outside.

A block later I stopped and stared in the window of a botánica crowded with artículos religiosos, bright-colored flowers and herbs, and statues of Jesus, saints, and fierce-looking deities I didn't know. A handmade sign advertised the prices of ducks, chickens, and female goats for sacrifices to the Santería god of the seas.

Two women dressed in white, wearing beaded bracelets, went through the front door. Brass bells on woven strings bounced against the glass, and heavy rosewood-smelling incense rushed over me in a thick pink cloud.

The door stayed open, as if inviting me inside. I stepped closer. Brass charms, candles inscribed with prayers, and packets of roots, leaves, and herbal remedies lined the walls behind the counter.

An old bent woman biting a thick cigar gave me a strange look and walked over to the entrance, the hem of her long yellow dress sweeping across the floor.

"Ah, you a bad one, you are," she said, the cigar wagging at the corner of her mouth as she spoke. "You got no future. No future on your face. None at all." She smiled and blew smoke into my face.

I breathed in the acrid smoke.

"You need a cure, I think. I could give you what you need. But you got to pay the price, eh?"

She slammed the door.

I stood looking at my reflection, wondering what she had seen in my face. That I was a murderer? Had forced my best friend onto the street and to her death? I felt suddenly hot even with the devil winds spinning down the street.

I waited to see if the woman would come back and say

more. When she didn't, I held my hand up to the glass to cut the reflection and peered inside the shop. She gathered some herbs and shook them into a pouch, her cigar making a halo of smoke over her head. She set the pouch on the counter, then glanced at me and laughed. She spread her arms and closed her eyes, her fingers stretching. She mumbled something over the pouch, then followed the women in white to a back room. I opened the door quickly, the bells chiming a warning, stole the pouch from the counter, and ran with it down the street.

At the corner I turned to see if the woman had come out. No one was there, and for some reason I didn't understand, I felt disappointed that she hadn't chased me down. I wondered if the old woman was only one of my dreams…but the pouch was real. I held it to my nose and breathed deeply, licorice and thyme smells filling my lungs. The puppy sniffed and licked the pouch until its nose was covered with a fine gray powder.

I walked two more blocks, then turned down the crooked sidewalk that led to the row of houses where I lived. Our house had belonged to my grandparents, but after they died, it passed to my mother. I know they worried about my beautiful mother, a late-in-life baby, who spoke such a strange mix of Quechua, Spanish, and English that when she went to school no one understood her. Some days I could still smell my grandmother's cooking inside our home, but mostly I smelled the salt of sweat and smoke from my mother's boyfriends.

When I got near the house, Mrs. Mulligan, our next-door neighbor, slammed out the front door of her small stucco house, holding a casserole with ragged blue potholders. Her three oldest sons were stretched under her old rusted Buick, their long legs and cowboy boots sticking out from beneath the chrome. They had come from Oklahoma years ago but still dressed as if they expected to find a rodeo in the Hollywood Hills.

"Kata, wait," Mrs. Mulligan called, her red hair trying to escape from the scarf tied tight around her wide head. Boxer, her towheaded toddler, peeked around her pink flowered muu-muu and waved two wet fingers at me.

"Don't speak to her," one of her sons said from under the car. "We got enough trouble with her without you starting more."

"I'm just asking how she is," Mrs. Mulligan said, her voice straining to sound cheerful.

"You just listen to us," another twangy voice came from under the car's radiator.

"Okey-dokey," Mrs. Mulligan said.

She handed me the dish. "It's a tuna casserole," she whispered. "I know it's your favorite. Well, you won't be able to eat today, but I wanted to do something."

I stuffed the sweet-smelling pouch into a pocket,

balanced the pup, and took the hot casserole in the soiled potholders, the fishy smell steaming into my face.

"I heard about your Ana," she whispered. "I'm sorry."

"Mom, are you still talking to her?" a voice said as the dolly's metal wheels scraped the driveway and one pair of legs grew a body.

Mrs. Mulligan hurried away before her son Judd could stand. He had a dark tan and deep blue eyes. He pushed a greasy hand through his blond hair and looked at me.

"You stay away from us," he said, pointing his wrench.

I ran around the cinder-block wall up to my house and hurried inside to hide the tears that were becoming stronger than my will to hold them back.

The wind followed me inside and rippled through the layers of cigarette smoke hanging in the living room. I set the casserole down on the coffee table before my fingers blistered, then cradled the puppy slipping from my arms and set it on the floor.

A silent television flickered in the corner, pictures changing rapidly, showing weather across the nation. The light made me think of the fire my grandparents had kept in the hearth. Grandma liked the soft noise of the crackling logs and the light of the licking flames, even though it was too hot most days in Los Angeles to have a fire. Mom must have missed the fire, too, because I had found her many times with her back to the TV, the sound off, her eyes watching the light change across the wall.

Mom was sleeping on the couch, blankets twisted around her limbs. I pulled the pouch from my pocket and set it near her pillow. I closed my eyes and said a silent prayer for a milagro, then touched her shoulder, her yellowed skin loose on her thin bones.

"Momma," I whispered, and breathed deeply, taking her exhaled breath into my lungs. I couldn't smell alcohol, and that made me hopeful that maybe she would keep her promise this time. But hope was a tool the devil used against me, tricking me into believing my mother's words.

I set the puppy on her lap. It startled her. Her eyes opened, black beads pushed inward by puffy lids. She looked at the little dog, her face blue-green in the jumping TV light. She leaned on an elbow and grabbed the puppy to keep it from falling off the couch. Pink fuzz from the blanket caught on the puppy's nose.

"I brought you a present," I said. "Someone to keep you company when I'm at school."

"I can't have a dog," she said. "How can we feed it? We don't got money for a dog. You take it back." That was what she said, but already she was letting it lick her ear. I smiled but didn't let her see my smile.

"What are you going to name it?" I asked.

"I can't keep it," she said, picking the fuzz from its nose.

Boxer peeked in the front door, his cheeks powdered with dirt, sucking on two fingers.

"There's your little crumb-snatcher Boxer, begging at the front door," Mom said, and kissed the dog's wet nose. "Better get him out of here before the Mulligans make stew of us." She laughed at that, but I never got her jokes. Then her voice got nasty-mean. "Go away, Boxer. Go away," she said like she was chasing flies.

"I'll take care of it," I said.

I took Boxer to the kitchen and wet a paper towel to wash his face. I liked the way he held his face up to me, eyes squinched closed, lips pursed. I let my hands linger on his face and gently washed his lips and finally behind his ears—the way I had always wanted my mother to touch me. Sometimes when I was a little girl, I would play with my mother's hand, pretending her hand was a doll. She'd let me hold the hand, kiss the fingers, cuddle the arm while she drank her beers and smoked with her free hand and talked to dark men. Playing with her hand was the only way I could feel her touch.

When I finished washing Boxer's face, I kissed his nose and gave him a roll of Life Savers. Boxer smiled. I think he liked my washing his face better than the Life Savers.

"Boxer, you better get out of here before your brothers come looking for you with a switch."

He sat down on the floor and worked his chubby fingers around the paper covering the candy. He opened it too far, and the Life Savers fell out and danced across the room.

"Boxer, you go on home," I said, helping him pick up the candy and stuff it into his pockets.

He smiled.

"Come on," I said. "I'll help you sneak out."

I walked him into the backyard. Too late. Judd was standing beneath the avocado tree. When he saw me with his baby brother, he spit fire.

"What are you doing with Boxer?" he said.

"I don't speak English," I answered.

"You bitch, you're speaking it now," he said.

"Yes, but these are the only words I know," I said calmly.

He was still calling me names when I locked the back door. I had broken into their home many times when I was younger, stealing milk, cereal, and coins. Mrs. Mulligan understood poverty and never held it against me. Whenever she could, she brought me plates of leftovers and cookies, but fear made Judd and his brothers close their hearts against me, fear that there wasn't enough to go around.

I took two plates and forks and a serving spoon into the living room. I scooped Mrs. Mulligan's tuna casserole onto the plates and handed one to Mom. I tried to eat, but my throat closed. How could I eat with Ana gone? I set my plate on the rug for the puppy. It waddled over to the plate and ate, its front paws slipping on the noodles, its ears gathering the sauce.

Then I remembered the vitamins.

"I bought you some vitamins today," I said. "I thought they'd make you feel better." I set the bottles of pills in a line on the coffee table.

"I can't swallow pills," Mom said. "So you shouldn't have wasted your money." She started to take another bite of casserole but stopped when she saw I wasn't eating.

"Nobody can eat after a funeral," she said, and set her plate down. "Three days since Ana . . . I'm sorry, baby. I just felt too weak to go to the funeral. We'll visit her grave . . . lay some pretty flowers there." Her fork dropped to her plate with a clank that echoed through the cold house. She stared off as if some other funeral played across the gray wall in the living room.

She pulled the blanket over her head, like she was trying to escape the demon memories. When she did, Nando's book fell to the floor with a dull thud, startling the puppy. Nando was a poet. He had won awards and had three books of poetry published. Four poems were about Mom. She read them again and again. I think she missed Nando. But her love wasn't strong enough to keep her from drinking.

Nando had put hope in our lives for a while. He wanted to marry Mom and make us his family, but then Pocho joined the gang and Mom started drinking heavy. She spent her nights walking the streets with Pocho's picture in her hand, trying to find him and pull him home. Her days she spent in bed with wine and beer, until one day Nando came home and found her sharing her beer and bed with a strange man. Nando left, and Mom didn't go looking for him. He called me sometimes, but he didn't visit. His heart was still soft in the center for Mom, and he was afraid to find her with another stranger.

I picked up the mail off the rug by the front door.

"You get your welfare?" I asked. Mom was disabled from the drinking, her liver turning to stone. She received SSI and an AFDC check for me as long as I stayed in school. I hated the welfare. Other kids, like some of the girls in the projects, didn't seem to mind the poverty the way I did. It felt like an anchor, keeping me down.

"Krandel came by," Mom said.

I glanced around the room. The smoke was thick. Too much smoke for Mom to have made with her thin, dry lungs. "You let that six-pack of trouble into our house and he took your welfare, didn't he?" My words were harsh, but my tone was resigned. I knew she had endorsed her welfare over to him. I didn't need to ask. She had done it too many times before because Krandel kept the drinks flowing when I refused to go to the market for her. Krandel took advantage of her, but he never beat her or tried to sex me like some of the others had.

"Mana yuyanichu," she said from beneath the blanket. I think that meant "I don't remember" in Quechua, but I wasn't sure. She could have been telling me to mind my own business.

I sighed. I didn't have the energy to battle with her. I had left it in the cemetery.

"Maybe Nando can help us," I said. How could I blame her anymore? Men and booze were the only way she forgot her sad, broken life. She had me when she was fifteen, and maybe that was the reason I stayed away from boys and didn't dream about babies the way the other girls did. I knew how bad it felt to have a mother who should have been an older sister.

She told me my dad was dead, shot in a drive-by. But I think she only said that so she could get her welfare and not bother him. I liked to think Nando was my father. Mom said he wouldn't be a good father because he practiced Santería, an old Afro-Caribbean religion brought to the New World centuries ago by slaves from the West African Yoruba tribe. Mom was Roman Catholic, so anything superstitious was bad to her. Nando was always bringing over a chicken for her to hold for him until he could sacrifice it. He teased her with the flapping bird, chasing her with the clucking chicken until feathers spun around the house and we were all sneezing and dizzy. I never saw him kill anything, though. He was too tender of heart and soft in his eyes.

They argued religion, Mom holding her rosary twisted in her hands, her face yellow in the light from the candles Nando had lit to his gods. Nando saw life as a complex thing of prayer and fate. God was so immense to him that he needed saints and lesser deities to do his bidding, like Mom and I prayed to Holy Mary and Jesucristo.

"They just put in a good word for me," Nando argued. "I'm not worshipping them."

I didn't see how anyone could fight over religion, saying one was right, the other wrong. It was as if people made gangs out of their religions. To me it didn't matter how a person got to God; getting there, that was the hard part, that was all that mattered. Mom couldn't think that way. Every time Nando did something that didn't please her, she blamed his religion.

"You stay away from Nando and that West Indian witch he lives with—Consuela, whatever her name is," Mom said, suddenly alive again. "She's put too many curses on me."

"His bruja is nice to me," I lied. I'd never seen his other woman, but Mom talked about Consuela all the time.

"Give him back his jewelry," Mom said.

Mom had an opal ring and earrings Nando had given her. She never wore them. When I asked why she didn't wear the jewelry, she said she was saving it for good. That made me think she saw a future for us outside the barred windows of my grandparents' home.

"Tell me about the funeral," Mom said finally. "No, don't. I hate funerals."

The changing pictures on the TV silently washed over her face with ghost lights. She lit a cigarette and offered it to me. I took a drag. It tasted bitter. She pulled the blankets back over her head before I could give the cigarette back to her. I put it out in the ashtray, then picked the puppy up and put it under the blanket with her.

I walked out to the front yard. Music came from a neighbor's house, soft and seductive. I hated the sound of it. My body wanted to dance, but it felt wrong without Ana. I sat on the cinder-block wall between the Mulligans' balding lawn and our stubby crab grass, watching the moon rise in the east, swinging my heels to the beat.

Mom and Nando had fought over the wall.

"There's no need for a wall there," Mom had said.

"Hate's a good reason," Nando had answered. The Mulligans' son Tyrone had called me a bastard. I didn't know what the word meant then, but words were important to Nando.

"Words bruise and batter on the inside," Nando had said. "Words hit deep in your heart so the bruises don't show and your skin doesn't bleed. Sometimes you're not even aware of the damage the words have done because you can't see the wounds."

I sat on the wall of hate thinking about that night.

Suddenly strong arms pushed me from behind. I fell forward and landed on our lawn. I turned quickly, ready to run around the wall and fight the Mulligan boys.

Instead Pocho stepped from behind the wall and stood over me.

"Let's go," he said. Pocho seemed agitated, his eyes deadened, and in the moonlight with the wind blowing dark shadows back and forth across his face, he looked frightening. He lifted his T-shirt and showed me the butt of a gun hidden in his waistband, tight against the tattoo of a weeping woman on his lean stomach.

"Do you know who to get?" I said.

He smiled, but the smile never reached his eyes.

"Yeah," he said. "I know who."

That was all I needed.

I sat in the front seat of Pocho's 1981 Oldsmobile Cutlass and took the gun when he handed it to me. It was heavy in my hands. My heart beat rapidly, thumping inside my chest as the car pulled away from the curb.

Judd was sitting on his front porch under the yellow beam of the porch light. He looked up as we rolled by. I pointed the gun at him.

"Pow," I whispered.

He went white with fear, and I liked the feel of power the gun gave me. I was in control now.

•   •   •

We drove to another neighborhood, cautious, low in our seats, watching the oncoming cars, knowing we were in enemy territory. We parked Pocho's car under the shadow of a low-hanging pine tree, then jumped out and ran to a Chevrolet Impala. I held the gun tight against my side. Pocho gripped a screwdriver in his hand and pulled his sleeve down over his fist. He broke the car window with a sharp blow and crawled in behind the steering wheel. He hit the ignition, knocking away the key lock, and started the car with the screwdriver. I slid into the car then, the pebbles of broken glass rubbing against me. We rolled away from the curb in the stolen car as a porch light came on in the house behind us.

"Hurry," I said.

Pocho turned the corner.

"They got any music?" he said, and started going through a stack of tapes on the front seat.

"Leave it," I said as I rolled down the window. "Watch the road."

My heart was pumping. I was ready, but Pocho was making me too nervous, like hot wire jumping through my skin, the way he was searching through the cassettes, clattering the plastic. He turned on the overhead light, read the titles one by one, and threw each out the window. Long lines of brown tape flew in the wind behind us.

"All they got is country-western," he said.

"Are we here to listen to music?" I said, and turned off the overhead light. I tore the tapes from Pocho's hand and started going through them, using the gun muzzle like a finger to separate them.

"Here. Patsy Cline," I said. "I like her." I pushed the tape into the cassette player and sweet sad music filled the car.

Pocho tried to rip it out. "I don't want something that's going to bring me down."

I hit his hand. "Leave it," I said.

Groups of kids stood outside on the sidewalk, backlit by the light from houses. Their heads turned as we passed, checking us out, the same way we watched cars in our neighborhood. No one seemed alarmed yet. I looked at the houses falling behind us. The shifting lights from televisions inside colored the front windows.

"It feels like a fire's burning inside me," I said, stroking the gun.

Pocho nodded.

"That guy shouldn't have capped her," I said. "Not Ana. She was just kicking it, keeping it real. She never did a drive-by, never hurt anyone."

"You ready?" Pocho said.

"Yeah." I was ready to shoot, eager to blast the guy who had killed Ana. "No one hurts Ana without hearing from me," I said, feeling the devil squeeze my heart. "No one."

"Here," Pocho said in a whisper, his voice straining with

anticipation. He stopped the car at the curb near three trash cans waiting for pickup. The foul smell of garbage crept into the car, but I couldn't roll up the window, not now, with our mission so close.

Pocho turned off the tape player and pointed to a wood house with a long porch. The porch was crowded with people old and young. A pink unicorn piñata hung from an oak tree in the front yard.

"Must be some kid's birthday," I said.

"Check out the car," Pocho said.

A Monte Carlo was parked in the drive. It could have been the one that drove by that night, the one used by the bangers who shot Ana, but I wasn't sure. A Monte Carlo is a gangbanger's dream car. Any GM car is. And maybe they had stolen a car, like we had, for their mission.

"There," Pocho said. "Coming out on the porch now. That guy."

"He's the one?"

"Yeah."

"You're sure?"

"Blast him."

Suddenly Pocho slammed on the gas and tires squealed, burning a path of rubber behind us, the back end of the car fishtailing.

"Do it. Do it!" Pocho shouted as we sped toward the house.

"You're crazy," I said. "There's all kinds of people on the porch, kids and old people. I'm not going to shoot and kill some baby."

"Shoot!" he shouted.

"No, not this way," I said. We sped past the house.

Pocho turned the corner tight, then stopped the car with a jerk. I fell forward and hit my head against the dashboard.

"Now they know we're here," he said.

"I don't care," I said, and opened the car door. "I'm not killing a baby. You take your busted self back home. I'll handle this. If somebody's going to get blasted for Ana, it's going to be the right somebody, not some baby or someone's grandmother."

I climbed out of the car and slammed the door.

"Get back in," he growled, and backed up the car, following me.

"No," I said. "I want to see him when I shoot him. I want him to see the pain in my eyes when he dies, not some anonymous flash from a car so that he doesn't even know what hit him. I want him to know it's me and that I'm here for Ana. I want him to know he's going to die."

"Get in the car!" Pocho yelled. "They know we're here. They'll be waiting for you."

I didn't care. I turned the corner and started walking toward the house, the gun in my right hand, muzzle pointing toward the sidewalk. A bougainvillea hung over the redwood fence near the house, and my feet crushed the fallen blossoms, staining the sidewalk red.

I could hear the people on the porch talking and laughing and teasing some boy.

I walked up to the front fence that was heavy with honeysuckle, the gun at my side.

"I'm here for Ana!" I yelled. "Chancey, you know her? Anybody here know her?"

They all stopped talking and stared at me.

The guy Pocho had pointed out said something to the others. Then he hopped off the porch into a line of purple azaleas, his feet sinking into the wet soil, and walked toward me, almost tripping over a green garden hose that stretched across the lawn. He ducked under the piñata swaying from the oak tree and stopped. He didn't dress the part. He looked like a college student in his blue T-shirt and Levi's. He wore a single gold earring, his black hair long and pulled back in a ponytail.

"I know Ana," he said, and looked behind him as if he was afraid the others might hear him. Then he whispered, "I'm Raul."

I didn't understand why he was telling me his name or why he seemed so worried that the people behind him would hear what he said. But it didn't matter.

"This is for Ana," I said, and drew the gun up to fire.

A woman on the porch screamed, "She's got a gun."

I could hear feet scuffling, mothers grabbing up their children and pulling them inside, footsteps running down the driveway to the back of the house.

I held the gun at him. He didn't move and he didn't look afraid. He smiled at me like this was a big joke. When I looked into his brown eyes, I saw Ana's eyes staring back at me with love. Suddenly the gun felt too heavy to hold. I lowered my arms.

"You don't have to be so dramatic," Raul whispered. "Just tell me where to meet Ana."

"You crazy?" I shouted.

"Hey, what's up?" a lazy voice said behind Raul.

Two vatos wearing sunglasses had jumped off the porch and strolled toward us. They wore black baggy shorts that hung below their knees and white socks pulled up to their knees and black tennis shoes. They kept their heads back and had the look. I knew they were strapped by the way their hands played under their T-shirts.

"Where you from?" asked one with the name Chucho tattooed across his neck.

"She's from nowhere," Raul said to them in a rough voice. "Stay back so I can talk to her."

Why was he trying to protect me?

"Hey, we just come to see what she's doing outside her neighborhood."

Raul took control. "Look, you guys, get back. I can

handle my own. This doesn't concern you. It's just between her and me."

He waited until they were back on the porch. They lit cigarettes and watched us with the coolness of death.

Raul turned back to me. "Where does Ana want me to meet her?"

Tires squealed. Pocho drove the car around the corner and stopped it behind me, engine racing, ready to escape.

"Come on," he yelled. "Shoot."

I lifted the gun again and clicked off the safety.

"Ana's in heaven and you're going to hell," I said.

He gripped the fence. The honeysuckle shook, making the air too sweet to breathe.

"Don't say that, even as a joke," he said.

My mind was whirling. I was too confused. The gun started shaking in my hand.

He spoke rapidly. "Ana said she was going to take a test."

"What do you care about her algebra test?" I asked, looking at him over the trembling barrel of my gun.

"Not an algebra test," Raul said. "A test to see if she was pregnant. I would have snuck over, but I had to go to Fresno to work the fields with my uncle. I couldn't send anyone to tell her, not in enemy territory. That's the only reason I didn't go over to find out. I wasn't running out on her. I hope she didn't think that. I want to marry her. She's my life."

"You trashin' liar." I spit out the words. "Ana wouldn't have gone with some guy out of the neighborhood. Not someone we hate."

A siren shrieked in the distance.

Pocho started screaming "Kata, Kata, Kata" in the car behind me. He repeated my name like an engine, pumping the words with a steady rhythm, trying to bring me back to him.

"You're Kata? Ana must have told you about me?" Raul said.

I shook my head.

"Tell her I'll sneak over tonight. After midnight. Tell her to leave her window unlocked."

"Ana's dead." The words felt miserable on my tongue.

He looked at me like he didn't understand.

"A drive-by," I said. "Some of yours shot her. The funeral was today."

Raul reached over the fence and grabbed my sweatshirt, his face churning with the blackness of a storm. Honeysuckle brushed against my face, the delicate blossoms filling my eyes.

"Tell me you're lying!" he roared.

I lifted my arms to push him away and remembered the gun. This was all too much for the vatos on the porch. They started firing.

Raul dropped to the ground. When he did, I fired back at them. The recoil smashed through my bones.

I fired and fired, the police siren sounding louder and louder, the thumping blades of a helicopter approaching rapidly, people in the house screaming.

I fired the gun until I had no more bullets, then stood there, still pulling the trigger, waiting for a bullet to find me and take me to Ana.

"Kata!" Pocho screamed. Suddenly his fierce hands pinched my arms and yanked me behind a tree. Pocho held me against him. I could feel his heart beating in his chest, his jagged breathing a wind against my ears.

When the shooting stopped, he pulled me out into the street. I started to go to the car, but Pocho jerked me back just as a beam of white light swept over it. We ran from the searching light of the helicopter to a house across the street and darted into the backyard. Protected by shadow, we climbed over a fence and ran down an alley, finally stopping to rest behind a line of trash bins on the next street.

I was crying. "I never shot at anyone before."

"Forget it," Pocho said. He took the gun from me, wiped it on his T-shirt, and tossed it into a storm drain. Then he grabbed my hand to make me run again.

"Forgive me," I kept saying over and over, like counting off Hail Marys on a rosary. "I hope I didn't hurt anyone. Please, God," I cried. "Don't let anyone be hurt."

Then the fog rolled in. It curled around the streetlights, absorbing sound and locking silence around us. Usually I enjoyed the damp heaviness of fog, but this was a strange neighborhood. Pocho pulled at me, and we hurried across the street. At the corner about twenty women held candles. The candle flames shimmered through the veil of fog. The women looked ghostly and unreal. In some neighborhoods gang fighting was so out of control that mothers made a human wall between war zones at night. They gathered and lit candles, trying to stop the killings.

I didn't like being so close to the border between two gangs' neighborhoods, both enemies to us, and I knew Pocho didn't either, because he took my hand and pulled me along, trying to make me run faster. We dodged into the next alley and clung to the shadows along the fence.

A police car drove down the cross street, and then I heard the thumping rotor blades from the sheriff's helicopter overhead. The helicopter's searchlight broke the foggy darkness and shone over the street like strange moonlight.

We crawled under a car parked on the next street. I lay there with my cheek resting in broken glass and dirt.

Pocho lay next to me. "Why didn't you shoot him?" Pocho said.

I told him what Raul had said about Ana.

"Not Ana," he said.

"Ana told me she was pregnant," I said.

"Then it was mine," Pocho said, but his voice told me he was forming a lie.

"I believe Raul," I said. "I saw his eyes."

"What does that mean, you saw his eyes?" Pocho said, his lips moving against the dirt on the street.

"My grandfather said true lovers share the same soul."

"So?"

"I saw Ana in Raul's eyes. They share one soul."

"So you fired at his house, and now they know your face and they'll all be hunting you down and the sheriff, too. Jesus, Kata."

"I couldn't kill Ana," I said. "He had Ana's eyes."

"Your grandfather had too much imagination, and so do you. You see things that aren't there all the time, so what makes you think this was any different? God, Dreamer, wake up."

"Raul told the truth," I said.

The helicopter light swung to another block. Pocho pulled himself from under the car and started running again. I followed him, my chest blazing with pain.

Pocho stopped. "It's safer if we split up," he said. "I'll go back the way we came. You go home."

"No," I said. I knew Pocho was going to try to draw them away from me so I'd be safe. I wasn't going to see another friend take a bullet because of me. "I'm staying with you."

Pocho pushed me hard and backed away from me. "We'll both be dead if we don't go different ways," he said.

"Come back," I wailed.

He threw our gang sign at me and took off running in the direction we had just come from. I knew I couldn't catch him. He was gone already.

I cut across the street and turned at the next corner, running, not looking back, my lungs choking for air, sweat beading on my cold forehead. Then I heard footsteps behind me. I turned, thinking Pocho had come back, but instead I saw a group of bangers running after me, fast and sleek like a pack of wolves, splitting up now to cover any direction I could run.

I let out a desperate cry and ran down the nearest driveway. I flung myself over the back fence and went down hard, landing on my hand. Splintered wood and dust fell into my face. I could hear pounding footsteps on the other side of the fence. I dived under a boysenberry bush, the thorns pricking my skin and cutting into my face. I froze and held my breath as the fence rattled against my back and the vatos flung themselves over and into the yard.

My muscles ached from holding so still, and my lungs grew hot from wanting to pull in oxygen. I closed my eyes tight so I wouldn't see the bullets coming.

A back porch light came on. The back door opened and a high, angry voice filled the night air. "Get out of my yard!"

"Bullshit," one of the vatos spit.

Then the man on the porch stepped aside and two pit

bulls ran into the yard. Rough shouts filled the backyard, and the vatos disappeared into the night, the dogs growling at their heels. I waited until I thought they were on the next block, then pulled myself up and started walking again, my twisted hand throbbing, the tiny boysenberry thorns digging into my temples.

When I finally got home, I tiptoed into the kitchen. I didn't think my heart was ever going to slow down. I wondered if Pocho got away safe.

I walked into the living room.

"Kata . . ."

A scream struggled up my throat, but I stopped it. Mom was sitting in the dark.

"What are you doing up?" I said.

"Waiting for my daughter." She had never waited up for me before—ever.

"No men to keep you busy?" I said. The empty space between us had grown too large for her to close it now by staying up late, waiting for me.

"You found those words pretty easy," she said. "Maybe you got more you want to say? Go ahead."

I shook my head, but I doubt she could see me in the dark.

She sighed and went to her room. I felt like I was watching her ghost. I wished she had loved me enough to wait up for me back when I needed someone to wait up for me, back when I still had a chance.

I went to my bedroom. I fell across my bed and drifted into a dream. Night dreams took me places I was always happy to go. But this half-waking dream kept me in my room, tied to the earth and all my troubles. The wind came into my dream, rushing around me with a great softness, whispering to me in a language I didn't understand, telling me of ancient and secret magic, trying to show me how to lift myself up and away from this life. I struggled to understand the words carried on the wind, but the answers remained lost in the wind's wailing.

A sound jolted me fully awake. I sat up in bed, listening, looking for the danger.

A shadow stood at my window. I sucked air into my lungs, expecting a spray of bullets to blast through the glass. Instead a hand reached up and knocked. I climbed from bed, went to the window, and pushed it open.

"Hey, Kata," Pocho said.

"You made it."

"Yeah, I run faster than bullets," he said, and smiled. "I got nowhere to sleep tonight."

"Come in, then," I said.

He swung his leg over the sill and pulled himself up and into the room. I closed the window and turned on the lamp on my nightstand.

Pocho sat on the edge of my bed, the springs sagging under his weight. His eyes looked blank and sad. He took off his shoes and let them drop on the floor. I lay on the bed and pulled the covers over me.

"You knew Raul wasn't the one who shot Ana," I said.

He nodded and took off his Pendleton and T-shirt. Tattoos covered the hard muscles on his back and arms.

"You took me to kill the wrong guy," I said.

"No," Pocho said. "I took you to the right one. I loved Ana. I did. You know? She never let me touch her, and then she goes off with some vato from another neighborhood. Raul's the one I wanted dead as soon as I heard."

"You should have blasted him yourself, then. It was wrong to send me."

"No, I couldn't. If you blasted him, people would think he killed Ana. If I did him, they'd believe the story and think Ana loved him and I was jealous. I wanted the secret to die with him."

"Who told you, anyway?"

"Amelia."

"The little bitch. Don't you mess with her."

"She caught Ana with Raul," Pocho said. "She knew about it but didn't tell me until after the funeral. Said she'd tell me about Ana if I let her in. She said you were keeping her out."

"She doesn't know what's up."

"Maybe I'll recruit her." He said it like a challenge.

"Don't mess with her," I repeated. "Out of respect for Ana. She didn't want Amelia in the life."

Pocho took off his jeans and fell back on the bed. He lifted one leg onto the mattress, then the other. I turned off the lamp. The light from passing cars and the glow from the neon sign of a taco stand on the corner lit the room, giving it a strange red cast.

After a while Pocho whispered, "Kata?"

"What?"

"I didn't mean to hurt the puppy." His words struggled from his throat. "What makes me do what I do?"

I shook my head against the pillow. "Why do any of us do what we do? We don't have many choices here."

"I didn't mean to," Pocho said, and stared at the ceiling. He was silent for a long time, and I thought he had fallen asleep, but then he spoke softly, his words filling the room with sadness. "I wonder if this is the way guys feel in war," he said. "I don't want to die."

"I know," I whispered. "I don't want to die either."

He took in a long breath and let it out slowly. "Why didn't she love me?"

I covered Pocho and put my arms around him. His skin felt cold, and he was shivering. I didn't think I could ever warm his body. Then I realized he wasn't shivering. He was crying like he had when we were little kids alone in the dark in my room. His sorrow scratched against his lungs and chest, sounding like a small bird trying to escape his body and soar to another world.

Knowing each other's hurts made us close but also drove us apart. It's hard to pretend you're strong around someone who's seen you at your weakest. Usually we needed to feel strong more than we needed each other.

Pocho pulled away from me. The movement was so sudden I thought he had changed his mind and decided to leave.

"I feel like someday I'm going to run past the edge into the darkness, and I won't come back," he said.

"You'll come back," I said. "You'll always come back."

He slipped his hands behind his head and stared at the passing car lights brushing the darkness across the ceiling.

"I can feel it waiting for me," he said. "Something black and ugly. It makes me jealous of that puppy."

"How can you be jealous of a dog?"

"'Cause I've been thinking about death, you know, 'cause of Ana, and I keep thinking about hell and what's going to happen to me when I die. That little puppy just dies. I mean, it's just gone and it doesn't feel no more when it dies, but me, I got to go to hell and spend eternity in flame."

"No, you don't," I said. "It's not your fault you live here. God knows that."

He paused and took in a deep breath, his chest rising

high under the covers. "Sometimes when I can't sleep, I go back in my mind to when I was three or four and I start living my life forward, thinking how different I'd do everything. Do you think I could have made anything different?"

"Things happen for a reason," I said. "Maybe we don't figure that part out until after."

"When we're with God."

"Yeah," I said.

"You know," he said, "I try to think of death like a phone call. Like I've just hung up with Ana. She's still there. I just can't talk to her because the connection is gone."

"Yeah," I said, feeling that dull pain in my chest again.

His shoulders shuddered, and he made a strange sound, a hiccup like he was trying to swallow back a sob. "But I don't want an invisible Ana," he said.

"I know," I said.

We lay in the dark a long time, not saying anything, watching lights and shadows change as cars passed outside my window.

Finally he spoke. "Kata, would you scratch my back?"

"Yeah," I said.

"Remember when we were niños?" Pocho said.

"Yeah," I said.

"You was so mean to me," he said.

"Yeah," I said. "I was mean to you."

"You taught me how to fight good," he said.

"It was the only way you were going to survive in our neighborhood," I said.

He was silent for a long time. "My mama was a lot like Ana. Do you remember her?"

"No," I lied, not wanting to remember the only time I'd met her.

I scratched his back until he fell asleep. Then I got up and looked out the window. The wind had scattered the fog, and the few remaining clouds looked white against an indigo sky. Shadows hovered close to the apple and avocado trees.

I had a strange feeling that something really bad was going to happen—worse than Ana's dying. I didn't know why I should feel so afraid. Nothing could be worse than losing Ana, but my hands started trembling and a lump I couldn't swallow grew in my throat. Nando said you can't miss something you never had, so there must have been a time when I felt safe.

I crawled back into bed, and when I glanced back out the window, I had the unshakable feeling that someone had been standing there, watching me. A small mark smudged the outside of the window like an angel's fingerprint.

My curandero grandfather had told me that in ancient times spirits and angels traveled in our world, but when people stopped believing in the spirit world, the door between the worlds closed. Now spirits and angels could only make the passage into our world by twisting through the keyhole and screwing their beauty into scary shapes: werewolves, vampires, and ghouls. Geists, my grandmother called these spirits that invaded our world.

My grandfather told me this when I was afraid of the invisible creatures I sensed lurking in the darkness around my bed. He protected me then, but now his power had faded into the black-and-white photographs that hung above my bed, and I didn't know who could protect me.

"Jesucristo, Redentor mío, ¿por qué me has desamparado?" I muttered, praying to God. "Why have you abandoned me?" But I didn't expect an answer. He couldn't hear me. I was lost to Him.

The next day I woke up alone. Ana was still dead. Pocho had left sometime during the night.

Sunshine turned the morning fog metallic and dusted the leaves with gold. Then the gold glare lifted and the fog disappeared the same way it had come, from nowhere and in silence like some mysterious force. It made me sad when the fog disappeared because I no longer had an excuse to stay in bed.

I got up and went to the kitchen, my bare feet cold on the linoleum floor, to make a cup of coffee for Mom. The faint smell of peanut butter and coffee lingered over the dirty dishes Pocho had left on the counter. Water dripped from the faucet onto a knife in the sink. I rinsed the dishes and left them on the drainboard, then boiled water and made a cup of coffee. I shook a vitamin from each of the jars and took the pills and coffee to my mother's room.

I pressed against the door. The room smelled sour, of stale love and beer and broken promises. The blinds were drawn against the sun. I crept inside to where Mom lay, tangled in her blankets.

Mom was awake and staring at nothing, her face pressed into her pillow. When I was a girl and she did that, I would run to her and shake her, afraid she was dead. Now some days I prayed for her to die because it was so hard to care for her, but then I would hate myself and pull back the prayer as if it were a kite sent out in a too violent wind.

I sat on the edge of the bed. I could feel the warmth and comfort of her body through the blankets. I wanted to crawl in bed with her and cry, but I was too afraid she might push me away.

The puppy was under the covers with her, its head bobbing, lifting the sheet as it shook the pouch I had stolen from the botánica.

"I'm sorry about the check," she said finally. "Krandel scares me."

I shrugged. "He scares me, too. He's a kuntur," I said.

That made Mom smile. I think kuntur means "bad-assed dude" in Quechua.

"You remember that Christmas you wanted the doll with the clown face and I wouldn't get it for you because I didn't like it?" she said.

I nodded.

"I gave you a Barbie," she said.

"Yeah, I remember."

"I wish I had bought that clown doll for you," she said, and looked away.

The puppy shook the pouch and the sweet smell of licorice and thyme filled the air.

"I'm sorry about a lot," she said.

"Forget it," I said.

"I thought I heard someone in the house last night."

"Probably the puppy," I said. "I brought you some coffee."

"Coffee?" She sat up in bed and placed the pillows behind her like a child on her birthday, playing princess.

She took the mug in her thin hands and sipped, steam rising to her face and circling around her eyes in a way that reminded me of the morning fog. Her face looked less swollen this morning, but her eyes still had a yellow cast.

"I hoped maybe Pocho had come home," she said.

"Take your vitamins." My words came out like jealous boots kicking dry cement. She looked at me curiously.

"Just try to swallow them," I said, my tone more gentle.

"If you can't, you can spit them out."

"In my coffee?"

I gave her the pills. One had stained the palm of my hand red. "If you can't swallow them, you can spit them back in my hand."

She put the vitamins in her mouth and swallowed them with the hot coffee, then looked up at me with a big smile. She had a beautiful smile but never seemed to use it, as if she had decided to put it away with the opals and save it for good.

"When you were born," she started, and looked away. Tears ran silently down her cheeks. When she saw me looking, she said, "My eyes are watering. It must be the hot coffee." I knew she was only trying to save me the embarrassment of her tears.

"What were you going to say about when I was born?" I asked.

"Nothing. Just a thought. It doesn't mean anything."

"I'd like to hear."

She stared off, and I followed her gaze, hoping to get a glimpse of what she saw the night I was born.

"I had different dreams of what our lives could be, but I lost them in the bottle. Then you came home all covered with blood and it felt like the night you were born. Like you could be reborn, and we could start again. I never meant to hurt you, Kata. Now I'm so weak I can't do much for you.

When I drink, I don't feel. Now I feel and I know I'm dying."

"Maybe the doctors can give you a new liver," I said.

"I'm no movie star." She laughed. "Sometimes I get a feeling that Nando's old Santería gods must have gotten so upset with me that they crossed the ocean from Africa and put a curse on me when I wouldn't marry him. That's when things turned from bad to worse, wasn't it? Sometimes I think I can hear those old gods dancing to the batá drums."

"Nando said the powers of the orishas can never be used to harm others," I said.

"I know what he said, but things weren't this bad then, were they? Even before Nando, it wasn't this bad."

"Things are fine," I lied. "Now that you've stopped drinking, you'll start feeling better."

She sipped her coffee and spoke into the cup like a child afraid of her mother. "I'm not supposed to have coffee either, am I?"

"I don't know," I lied.

She shrugged. "It'll be better for you when I go," she said.

"No, it won't," I said. "It won't."

"I'm going to an AA meeting," she said. "They got them at the church."

I had heard her say that before.

"Nando's taking me," she said as if that would give her words the force of truth.

"Nando?"

"I called him last night." She set the cup of coffee on the nightstand.

"What about that bruja he lives with?"

"She didn't answer, so I didn't hang up."

"She doesn't care if Nando sees you?"

"I didn't ask. He's going to take me out to County General, too. Let the doctor check my liver again."

"Good," I said, but we both knew it was too late even if she did stop drinking now.

She smiled, closed her eyes, and started to fall asleep. I took her hand and held it against my cheek. It felt cold and smelled of rose-scented lotion. I kissed the tip of each finger, then tucked the hand under the covers next to the puppy.

I dressed in jeans, a T-shirt, and a Pendleton and went outside. I knew the guys from last night would still be looking for me. The streets near my home wouldn't be safe, so I walked over to Kikicho's house. His house was at the dead end of a street near the graffiti-covered wall surrounding the old cemetery. I stared at the desperate rows of gray and white granite markers. Square gray buildings in the projects on the other side of the cemetery gave the illusion that the cemetery continued forever.

Kikicho was sitting on his porch reading a book. A line of half-empty Coors bottles, drowned cigarette butts in each, caught the morning sun and shot amber lights across the porch. The smells of onions, jalapeños, tomatoes, and hot oils came from the kitchen.

"I heard what happened," he said. "Pocho came by. He said those guys in the Monte Carlo have been out scoping the neighborhood, looking for you."

Kikicho had washed his blue-black hair, and it curled around his ears, still wet, dripping onto his white T-shirt.

I didn't know until I was sitting next to him staring at the graves that I had decided to let him own me.

"Get me pregnant," I whispered. "So I can face out and get my welfare."

He kissed me, then ran the tip of his tongue along my lip, his mouth tasting of toothpaste.

"I can't," he said.

"Why not?" I asked, kissing him hard.

He pulled me onto his lap, and his canes clanked to the porch floor with a hollow sound. "Because you always told me that's what you were running away from," he said. "That's the life your mom had, and you wanted something more."

"I changed my mind," I said. "I'd be better than her . . . At least she's alive . . ."

He let his hand touch the back of my neck, and then he tugged my hair, wrapping his fingers in it. I didn't want him to ever stop. He lifted my hair and kissed the side of my neck, then my ear.

He was silent for a long time.

"You got bigger plans than even you can see right now. And someday, no matter how much you love me, you'll have to leave me here," he said, his voice as soft and quiet as angel wings. "I used to want to ask you to take me with you, but I know I don't belong there, wherever it is. I belong here."

I wondered what he saw in me that made him think I could ever get out of here.

"The place I'm going, you don't want to go to," I said. "I wouldn't be a friend to take you along."

He looked at me funny. "Where's that?"

"Wherever God puts his fallen angels," I said.

"Listen, Kata," he said. "I'm getting out. They got a special program for people like me. I'm going to be one of those gang-intervention guys. Homies don't listen to anybody but homies, so maybe they'll listen to me."

I nodded, but I felt wounded inside. "You're going to desert me, too," I said in a voice so soft I wasn't sure I had spoken the words aloud.

"Let me do it with you."

He looked at me, his eyes serious, and I knew he was saying good-bye.

"Maggie is going to do it with me," he said.

"What? Maggie? You and her?" I said, feeling a new hurt fill the wound in my chest. I got up from his lap and started pacing.

"I'm sorry," he said.

"And I came here like a fool chavala asking you to get me pregnant. How did it happen?" I asked.

"We just started talking after you left me at the field."

I remembered how badly I had disgraced him by not going back when he called my name.

"Maggie's good," I said.

"I'm sorry," he said. "But you don't need me. You're going to do something big with your dancing. That's your future. You should stop doing it for nothing."

"No. I can't dance anymore. I picked some bad music," I said, remembering what Ana had said.

"Pues, change the music," he said.

"Too late," I said.

"Kata, dancing . . . it does something for you I can never do. I seen you onstage. You go someplace."

"That was with Ana," I said.

I left the porch and started walking. At the curb I stopped and turned back.

"Maybe you can tell the kids about Chancey and Dreamer?" I said.

"Yeah, I'll tell the girls about Outrageous Chaos," he said. "But I'll tell them not to be that way. It's too big a price to pay."

A garbage truck stopped where I stood. My lungs filled with the sour stench and exhaust. The garbage collector lifted a can, and I stepped back to avoid being thrown in, too.

I walked down the street, then through the county housing project to the old flood-control channel by the river. Serena was there, standing near a fire, dressed like a hoochie mama in tight shorts and a halter top, swaying to music from a boom box. Her eyes were glassy, reflecting the red flames, and I knew Pocho had stood her up already. She had a large brown bag next to her feet. When she saw me, she lifted a forty from the bag.

"Want one?" she said, her words slurred. She tried to smile, but her lips couldn't curl over her hurt.

"Thanks," I said.

She sniffed and threw a piece of wood on the fire. "It's cold," she said.

"Maybe you're coming down with the flu," I said to give her a reason to leave. I knew she wanted to go so I wouldn't see her cry.

"Yeah, maybe I better go home," she said, and handed me the bag of forties.

When she left, I tried to dance to the hard-hitting music coming from the boom box.

It was no use. My legs felt lifeless, and I twisted my ankle.

I sat by the fire getting sloshed on Olde English Malt liquor, waiting for the guys in the Monte Carlo to come find me in the puddles and foul-smelling black mud.

When the sun set, my homies started showing up. I watched them down forties and tequila and drag on passed-around weed, talking and flirting. But when Pocho came and started telling big stories about what we had done the night before, I left and walked home, the sour taste of alcohol on my tongue, my stomach stinging and wanting food.

Nando was sitting on our front porch, waiting for me, a chicken clucking in a wire cage next to him. His long black hair was thinning, and the breeze blew it up and down. His wire-rimmed glasses fell to the end of his fat nose when he stood. He pushed them up with his thumb, then opened his arms to me.

"Come here, mi'ja," he said in a soft voice that comforted me.

I fell against his thick body, his sweater scratching my cheek. He rocked me back and forth, and the smell of his tobacco and spicy aftershave made me cry.

"I'm sorry, baby," he said. "I'm sorry about Ana."

"Does Mom know you're here?" I asked finally.

"I didn't want to wake her," he said.

I knew he was afraid he'd find her in the arms of another man.

"She called you?"

"Yeah, to take her to the doctor and the AA, but mostly she was afraid you might do something . . . foolish," he said.

"Do what foolish?" I said.

"Nothing you do will bring Ana back. Don't throw away your life."

I pulled away from him. "This life?"

"You don't know what's coming," he said. He sat on the porch and patted the cement step for me to join him. "Maybe something good's coming in your future. Something you can't see yet because you're living too close to the earth."

"I know what's coming," I said. "I see it every day."

"It doesn't have to be that way." He raised his head and nodded toward the sky. "Look out there at all those stars hanging in that cold, vast heaven. It makes me feel like I'm standing on the edge of eternity."

I looked up at the sky and wished I could see what Nando saw. I only saw the red neon sign from the taco stand and pale gray clouds moving across a moonless sky.

"I always feel less burdened after star watching," he said. "Looking up at the stars gives me some perspective."

"Your words don't mean much to me," I said. "I got to keep my eyes on the street so I don't get shot."

He put his large arm around me. "Look up, Kata," he said. "The heavens give us a measure of what God might be: large enough to hold a billion trillion stars."

He drew me close to him, trying to guide my vision, until we were cheek to cheek, gazing at the night sky, his glasses pinching my temple.

"Don't look at the earth for the center of life," he said. "If you look up at the night and see what's above you, a lot of the things that bother you here aren't worth the fuss."

"Ana was."

"Ana was, but killing some vato for killing her, that's going to ruin your life."

"That's not what my heart feels," I said. "And you always told me to trust my heart."

His hand reached up as if he were trying to brush the clouds away so I could see better.

"There was a painter once who understood the power of the night sky. Vincent Van Gogh. You heard of him? He wrote to his brother Theo that when he had a need for religion, he'd go out at night and paint the stars."

I stood suddenly, unable to hold back my anger.

"Smog!" I yelled with a fury I didn't understand. "We don't see stars in this neighborhood. There's nothing in the night sky here but sheriff's helicopters and pollution."

I ran into the house, knocking against the chicken's cage. The chicken clucked and spread its wings. I slammed the door behind me. I could hear the door open and Nando's easy steps cross the carpet.

"Look around you, Kata. Look harder," he said with an anger that matched mine. "We're not here just to eat and sleep and breathe and die."

"How do you know?" I yelled back at him, and slammed my bedroom door.

"All right, you stay here in your pinche little neighborhood with your little life measured out in city blocks."

Then his voice came through the crack, sweet and gentle. "Dreams carry us, Kata. If you can't imagine yourself doing something other than living the life, then you won't do it. You've got a gift, Kata. Don't waste it."

I opened the bedroom door and looked at him. "I can't dance without Ana."

"Yes, you can," he said.

Nando wrapped me in a hug. I cried in his arms for a long time. When I stopped crying, he said, "You're right, Kata. There is too much smog in Los Angeles. If your mother's feeling well enough, I'll take you up to the mountains tomorrow night so you can see the night sky the way God meant it to be seen."

I nodded. "Okay," I said.

Nando slept on the couch, the chicken in the cage beside him, head tucked under its wing. During the night Mom got up and took him to her room. Her love sounds were different with Nando. The sighs they made were soft and sweet enough to bring babies from heaven. I sat there in the dark listening, even though I knew it was wrong, wondering if I would ever hear love sounds like that. And if I'd be able to hold on to it if I did.

Finally I could bear it no longer. I couldn't stand the thinking, the memories. I needed to run wild with the wind. I crept out of the house and walked down the street, watching each passing car. There was another battle of the go-go's at the Sports Arena. I caught a bus and went down there.

The crowd was huge, and I didn't know as many people as I had at the warehouse. I watched the girls go onstage in tight silk go-go shorts and gold high heels. I hadn't bothered to change my clothes. I wore my bagged-out jeans, Pendleton, and T-shirt.

When it was my turn, I went onstage without Ana, without a costume, without the honeysuckle. I felt like nothing. Guys started hooting when they saw me walk out. They threw beer. Foam splattered all around me. I held my head high and waited for the music to start. Then I rolled my hips. I rubbed my hands up over my body and into my beer-wet hair. The rain of beer stopped when I moved. I kicked out of my shoes and undid my belt. The bagged-out jeans fell to the floor.

The guys screamed. I guess they thought they were getting a show.

My jeans lay in the middle of the stage. I kept swinging my hips, moving my feet, unbuttoning my Pendleton. I let it fall slowly, like a snake shedding its skin. Then I traced my hands up my body again and into my hair, dancing with the music, my hips like waves on the ocean, my hands becoming the seagulls in the sky, and slowly the jagged edges of my world became smooth and liquid and I became the music. There was silence as I danced slow and sensual in my T-shirt and panties and bare feet.

The motion touched my heart, stirring a longing inside me that made me want to soar above my life and the violence to something good inside me that I had left with God.

The music stopped.

For a moment there was no sound. Then came booming applause that sounded like gunfire and made me feel like Ana on the corner, waiting for her bullets.

"More," people shouted. They wanted me to dance again, but I picked up my clothes and ran offstage. I stood trembling in the harsh light of a bare bulb encased in a steel frame. A tall, thin man handed me a beer. I took it and swallowed, finishing it. I wiped foam from my mouth and looked in his bloodshot blue eyes, set under heavy brows that joined at his nose.

He rubbed my side. "You want to give me a private party?" he said, and then he grinned at me, his smile a brutal slash across his gabacho face.

"Yeah, maybe," I said. "Get me more beer."

"How much do you want?" he said.

"Enough to carry me away."

"I got some tequila in my car," he said, and let his hand slip around my waist. He pulled me against him and walked me out into the cold. I still hadn't put on my clothes. He kept rubbing my side, inching up my T-shirt, until his hand was on my bare skin, dipping down in my panties, holding my hip. We wove in and out of the crowd that had gathered outside.

Kids were shouting their gang names, and fights were starting. Security guards were running, speaking into their radios, trying to stop the fights before they became a riot.

"What's your name?" I said as he opened the door to his Chevrolet Impala. "I want to know your name."

"James," he said, and I crawled into his car. He leaned over and started kissing me. I pushed him away.

"James, you promised me a drink," I said.

He pulled a bottle of tequila from under the front seat. He handed it to me, and his hand started sneaking up my T-shirt. I held his wrist and swallowed, tequila burning my throat.

Then shots rang out and everyone ran, their screams echoing in the night air. Bullets cracked and ricocheted off cement, as rapid as castanets. I fell to the floor of the car.

A shot hit the windshield and pebbly pieces of glass rained over me.

When the gunfire stopped, James held his shoulder, blood rushing through his fingers. I looked out the broken windshield. A Monte Carlo swerved and rammed into a police car as it turned the corner. Then it flipped and caught on fire.

I grabbed my clothes and the tequila and ran blindly away from the chaos. I found myself in a field and looked around frantically, too drunk to get my bearings. Finally I lay down where I was and fell asleep, a piece of driftwood, tossed and worn and washed up alone, far from home.

It was probably because of all the drinking the night before and sleeping in the field, and on top of that the hot bus and the closeness of the women pressing against me on either side, that I fell asleep on the ride home. When I woke up, my cheek rested on the bare shoulder of an old woman. A moist unwashed odor rose from her body.

I lifted my head. The sweat between her bare shoulder and my cheek made a sucking sound as I pulled away. She wore a faded red sundress with yellow flowers around the hem. The soiled straps of her bra dangled on her wrinkled arms. Her hair was wrapped in a careless bun on top of her head.

"You been partying?" she asked, the awful sour smell of her breath curling over me.

I said yes just so I wouldn't have to say anything else.

"I used to party," the woman said with a lopsided grin.

Her orange lipstick seeped into the tiny wrinkles that gathered like scars around her lips. "I partied every night. And fought, too. I kept a razor blade in my beehive hair. Sometimes I kept my boyfriend's knife there, too. The boys, they liked me real fine, you know what I mean?"

I nodded and stretched my arms.

"Every night," she said, and broke a banana from the bag of groceries caught between her swollen and scaly bare feet. The toenails were yellow and long, and I wondered if she had climbed on the bus barefoot.

When she finished peeling the banana, she gave me half. I said, "Thank you," and took a bite. Only then did I realize how long it had been since I had eaten. My head pounded, and I closed my right eye against the pain.

"I was a real good dancer." She sighed with her whole body, and I was afraid that if I encouraged her, she would start telling me intimate details from her past that I didn't want to hear. I looked at the front of the bus.

"Ay," she groaned. "A good dancer but the wrong music."

She kept moving her lips as if someone, visible only to her, had come up and starting arguing with her. Then I realized she was singing, her yellow plastic rose earrings flopping against the wrinkled skin on her neck.

Her eyes looked out the window, then darted back at me. "What music did you choose, eh?"

I didn't know what to tell her.

"Never mind. I know. I know the beat." Her feet tapped the floor, and her arms and shoulders moved with surprising grace. "Yeah, I know it, don't I? You never forget that dance."

She stood and pulled the line for the next stop, her body odor washing over me like dark waves and making my stomach turn. She pushed her swollen feet into worn yellow shoes that were hidden under the seat.

She smiled at me as I stood to let her out.

"Every night I partied. Every night. I was a real party girl, teasing all the boys and thinking I was so smart to make them all crazy over me." She smiled, chunks of banana caught in the folds of her wrinkled chin. I brushed them away with my hand, the saliva and banana making my skin creep.

"You'll see," she said, and stepped off the bus.

The bus jerked forward, pulling away from the curb. I felt suddenly cold and alone. It was as if a dark wind from somewhere in my future had blown the old lady to me. I stood and pulled the line for the next stop.

I jumped off the bus and ran back a block, past flower shops and women selling tamales from white kettles set on cardboard boxes, to find the old lady. I had to ask her what she would have done differently.

I stood there on the corner in the smogged air, traffic creating a wind of exhaust whipping around me.

The old lady was gone.

Three little boys were riding tricycles up and down the street. I stopped one with thin arms and a T-shirt that reached to his knees. His cowboy boots were worn and scuffed.

"Where'd the old lady go?"

He stopped pedaling and looked up at me with his brown eyes.

"You know, the old lady who got off the bus, what way did she go?"

He shook his head.

A woman slammed out of the house behind me. Her metallic red hair was wrapped in pink sponge curlers, and her face was covered with beauty cream. "What do you want with my son?" she asked.

"An old lady got off the bus," I said. "I need to talk to her. Did you see which way she went?"

"No old lady got off the bus," she said. She stepped in front of her son, her body a barricade to shield him from me. "The bus didn't stop here."

"It did. Just a minute ago. She was wearing a red sundress and yellow shoes."

"I've been watching the whole morning," the woman said, and folded her fat arms across her chest. "I should know. The bus didn't stop here."

I started running then, trying to outrun my thoughts,

but my mind was thick with words. Party girl . . . razor blade . . . that beat . . . that dance . . . wrong music . . . wrong.

I ran. But how do you run away from the future?

When I got back to the neighborhood, I saw Amelia standing with Pocho. She was dressed like some tough little chola in Converse sneakers with fat laces, low-slung work pants, her midriff bare, a gold hoop pinching the skin above her navel. She was going to let Pocho own her. I had seen that look on young girls before. He lit two cigarettes in his mouth at the same time, then handed one to Amelia. She took it and breathed deeply, the ember turning red.

"She's too young to smoke," I said to Pocho. Then I turned to Amelia. "What are you doing out here?"

She shrugged and bit a hangnail, then sucked the blood, the cigarette ember dangerously close to her eye.

"You stupid little chavala. You want Pocho to bust up your life like he did to Ana?"

She looked up at Pocho. He glared at me.

"You should be home studying," I said.

"Yeah, I gotta go," Amelia said.

She ran down the street. From the back it looked like Ana running away from me.

"Leave her alone, Pocho," I said. "I told you to leave her alone."

"It's her choice," he said.

"You want her to end up like some old lady on a bus without ever living her life?"

"You're crazy," he said. "You know that? You're crazy." His hand was shaking with anger, and ashes flew off the end of his cigarette, little gray specks floating around him like moths.

"Me? You said you loved Ana, but yesterday you left Serena crying down at the field, and now you're going after Amelia. You didn't love Ana."

"I loved her," he said, and his eyes went dead, the lids closing halfway.

"Just stay away from Amelia," I said. "Or I'll . . ."

"You'll what?" he said.

"I'll tell everyone about your mother," I said, and let my eyes meet his in challenge.

He stepped closer to me, and I could feel the muscles tensing inside his body, see the rapid pulse beat against the skin in his temple.

"I been with Amelia already, you bitch."

"You pig!" I yelled, and pushed hard against his chest. "No wonder Ana didn't love you."

His backhanded slap spun me around. But I swung, too, and connected. Blood trickled from his nose.

That made him really angry. He pushed me away and pulled a knife, the blade long and sharp. Sunlight reflected off the blade in white spikes.

I dumped a trash can, then kicked through the trash looking for a bottle. When I didn't find one, I dumped a second trash can. A beer bottle rolled into the street. I picked it up and hit it against the curb.

It didn't break. In the movies bottles break easily. In real life they don't. I swung it again as Pocho circled with his knife. He smiled and waited for me to come after him, his crystallized hate flowing out like icy breath from his lungs.

Finally the bottle broke, cutting my hand. I started after him, holding the neck of the broken bottle, my blood pattering on the sidewalk, curb, and street.

I glanced at the drops of blood and stopped, suddenly remembering Ana being carried to the ambulance. I looked up at Pocho, at the anger in his eyes. I had a choice.

"I'm not going to fight anymore, Pocho," I said. "You want to hurt me because I know your story. You think killing me keeps your past hidden forever? You can't hide it from yourself."

He swiped his knife across my stomach in three quick strokes back and forth, testing me. It didn't hurt, but I looked down and saw blood seeping into my torn Pendleton.

I dropped the bottle and stood there in the street remembering the day ten years ago when Pocho's mother brought him over to our house. My mother had just broken up with one man and had taken up with the first in a long line of other men. That new daddy was Pocho's father, and his mother went half-crazy when her husband left her for my mother.

I had opened the door, and she pushed Pocho at me.

"Give him to your mother," she said to me. "He comes with my husband."

Pocho ran after her.

"I don't love you anymore," his mother had said. "Go with your father and his whore."

She left Pocho crying on the porch. I wrapped my arms around Pocho, trying to keep him from crying, because I knew if his crying woke my mother, she'd be angry. But Mom wasn't angry when she woke up. She held Pocho and kissed his tears and rocked him the way I had longed for her to hold me. The more remote he was, the more my mother loved him.

Then one day, when he was eleven, the street became stronger, and the gang stole Pocho from my mother's love. He hid guns in the house and snuck out at night. He sprayed graffiti on the walls inside the house, and quit going to school. Mom walked the streets at night looking for him, but he was practically unrecognizable to her now.

I hated Pocho because Mom didn't go looking for me when I joined the gang. I hated Pocho because Mom gave him my kisses and they weren't good enough for him. But now, looking at Pocho, I saw for the first time that my mother's kisses had meant nothing. She was just a woman to him. It was the kisses from his own mother that he missed, and the absence of them had made him mean and angry.

"I'm not going to fight you," I said. "I don't want your kind of life anymore."

He looked at me like he didn't believe me.

"I'm done, Pocho. The life is killing us, and I don't want it," I said. "I'm sorry for your mother leaving you. I'm sorry you cry over it."

His eyes darted around like an animal caught in a cage looking for escape. I was telling the one thing he didn't want told.

"She didn't mean it when she said she didn't love you anymore," I said. "She couldn't have meant it. Maybe you should try to find her." I turned and walked away from him, my hands filling with blood.

People had come out of their homes and were standing at their gates. No one bothered to help me. They were too afraid of Pocho. I didn't blame them. He had too much hate in his eyes, and his reputation was too big.

"You're loca," he yelled after me.

"I'm sorry," I yelled back.

Tears were coming down my face now, and I didn't know if I was crying for me or the old lady on the bus or for Ana or Pocho or maybe for us all. I felt like the tears were making a river, and if I could find a boat, it would carry me to some distant, better place downriver.

I stopped in an alley to look at my stomach and see how bad it was. Then I walked to Harbor General Hospital and went to Emergency.

A doctor sewed up my stomach.

"Well, my mother never taught me how to embroider," she told me as she laid gauze over my stomach. "So I'm afraid the name tattooed across your stomach is going to look like hieroglyphics now."

"That's okay," I said. "It's not who I am anymore anyway."

She gave me a white envelope. "Take one of these pills every four hours for the pain. Keep the stitches clean and dry. Don't take baths. Showers only."

When she finished bandaging me, she stopped a nurse. "Will you find her some clothes she can wear home?"

The nurse took me to a storage room and found a pair of green slacks and a yellow sweater. I pulled them on and looked at myself in a thin mirror.

"You look like a regular kid," the nurse said. "We got a program to take the tattoos off with a laser if you're ever interested. It's free to gang members who quit the life."

"Thanks," I said.

As I started to leave, she handed me the bagged-out jeans, Pendleton, and T-shirt.

"Don't forget your clothes," she said. "They'll wash up, and you can sew the tears."

I looked at my clothes, rolled together like an abandoned cocoon.

"Burn them," I said.

I swallowed one of the pills and started to walk home, but as I passed the botánica, the fierce eyes of a ceramic saint caught the sun, and the reflection bore through me. I stopped and looked in the window, past the dangling charms, beaded necklaces, statues, and incense.

Something drew me inside. I opened the door slowly so the bells wouldn't give me away. The air was thick with gray smoke from burning tobacco leaves. Drums beat steadily, as rhythmic as the Sacred Mother's heart.

I crept past a line of brown coconutlike heads. Their shell eyes seemed to watch me as I stole to the back of the store, where the woman who had made me the pouch stood at a small altar decorated with seashells, starfish, and coral. The old woman bent and touched the floor with her hand, then kissed the dust on the tips of her fingers and placed a basket of red grapes in front of a statue of a beautiful black woman dressed in a blue robe the color of the sea.

"Buenas días," I said to her back.

"You come to me for revenge?" she said without turning, her voice low and angry.

"No," I said.

"The boy who shot your friend, his badness will make his own downfall."

"I didn't come for that," I said.

She turned and stared at me until the force of her gaze made me blink. Then she walked behind the counter. At first I thought she was going to go in the back room and leave me, but instead she struck a match. The flame flickered. She held it between us for an instant, then picked up a cigar and put it between her lips. She lit the cigar, took a long draw, and blew more smoke into the room.

"Why do you come, then?" she said, and lit a blue candle with the same match. She dropped the burning match into a small seashell.

I was afraid to say the words that tickled at my tongue.

She picked up the candle and held the flame in front of my eyes.

"You come here to show off the pretty future you got written all over your face now?"

My hands went up to my cheeks. My sudden movement made the flame jump. "You see a future?"

"Go home," she said, and set the candle back on the counter. "You don't need me."

She smiled at me and then she was laughing.

"Thank you," I said.

"I don't do nothing for you," she said. "You're never so lost that God can't find you."

"Thank you anyway," I said, and ran outside, the bells on the door clanking after me.

My feet started dancing faster and faster down the sidewalk. I leaped over two little girls drawing with chalk on the cement. Their heads jerked up and they looked at me. I smiled at them and jumped, pulling my arms tight to my chest, doing a complete rotation in the air.

"Wow!" one of the girls said.

When I landed, hot pain seared through me, but it was worth the smiles on their faces.

They dropped their chalk and ran to me.

"Do it again," one said, and looked up at me with a huge smile.

"What's your name?" I asked.

"Mila and Bella," the girl said, unable to say her name without calling the name of her friend.

Blackness washed over me. What good was a future without Ana?

I turned and started walking, pressing my hand against the stitches. The little girls ran after me, their shoes scuffing the sidewalk as they leaped and jumped. I couldn't stand the sound of their giggling. It made my heart think I could turn back and see Ana dancing after me.

When I got home, Mom was sitting in the backyard, her face yellow from her disease, a big sunbonnet on her head, the brim flopping in the breeze, her hands up to her elbows in a bucket of hot water. Feathers danced around her face and settled like new snow around her. The puppy chased and barked at the feathers.

Mom looked up, and when she saw me, she crossed herself, then closed her eyes as if she was saying a silent prayer. Finally she said, "Where have you been?"

"I'm sorry," I said.

"Thank God you're safe," she said, and brushed a feather settling on her face.

"What are you doing?" I asked.

"I'm making dinner." She smiled and pulled the carcass of the chicken she was plucking from the steaming water. "You remember the jalapeño chicken that Abuelita used to make?"

"Yeah," I said, and sat down watching her.

When she had finished plucking the chicken, I said, "Mom, how come you loved Pocho more than me?"

"What?" She lifted the chicken from the water like a newborn.

"You always held him and hugged him and gave him kisses that I wanted."

"You didn't need me," Mom said. "You were always cleaning and helping and silent like you had nothing to say to me. You had your own world from the day you were born, and I thought you were happy with it. Pocho had nothing but tears."

"I kept my tears inside me," I said. Then I told her about the old woman on the bus.

She nodded. "When I didn't find you home this morning, I took the last pennies from the teapot and went down to the church and lit candles. I prayed to Blessed Mary to take pity on another mother. Somehow I knew you were going to be okay, so I came home, and, well, this is what I did so we could have a dinner. There's not much food in the house."

"You knew I was coming back?"

"I felt it in my heart."

She came to me and gave me a kiss. Her breath smelled of coffee, and that smell made my heart so happy my mind started spinning a good future for all of us.

"Where did you get those clothes?" she asked finally.

"The hospital," I said, and lifted my sweater.

She drew in air in a long hiss.

"I'm done, Mom," I said. "I quit the life."

She wrapped her frail arms around me. I tried to hug her back, but my body felt stiff from the stitches and pain.

"Go lie down while I make dinner," she said, and puckered her lips for another kiss.

I awoke to the smell of chicken frying and went into the kitchen. Mom had set the table with Grandma's white china, then lit candles in old seashells and set them around the room. Her hair was long and waving down her back.

She kept pushing it behind her ears to show off the fiery opal earrings.

Nando came through the door and smiled awkwardly like he was meeting us for the first time. His collar was wrinkled as if he had tried on a tie, taken it off, and tried it again before finally deciding against it.

We sat at the table. Mom placed a platter of fried chicken in the center of the table and poured a glass of water for each of us.

"I don't have anything else to serve," she said. "No vegetables."

Nando took a big bite.

"This is the best chicken I've ever tasted," he said. "It doesn't need anything else."

I took a bite, the peppers burning my lips and tongue. "It's just like Grandma's," I said.

Mom smiled and sat down, spreading a linen napkin across her lap. "Now, doesn't it make more sense to use those poor chickens for dinner than to sacrifice them to some Santería god?"

Nando looked at my mother. Then he looked at me.

His mouth dropped open and the bite of chicken fell out.

"You killed Consuela?" Nando cried.

"Consuela?" Mom looked from him to me and back at Nando. "Your bruja?"

Nando put his hands over his eyes.

Mom spit her bite of chicken onto her plate. She understood in a flash of clarity that Nando had never had a West Indies girlfriend, only a pet chicken named Consuela.

"I didn't see it was always the same chicken. I was too drunk to see." She kissed him and stared into his eyes. "Too drunk to see the truth."

She left the room and came back with a soup tureen. She placed her linen napkin in the bottom of the tureen, then piled the fried chicken inside.

"Get the shovel," Mom said.

I met Mom and Nando at the corner of the yard, under the avocado tree. Mom nodded, and Nando dug the hole.

Mom placed the soup tureen in the hole, then took the shovel and worked until the hole was filled. I think Consuela was the only chicken of Nando's ever sacrificed.

"Come on," Nando said. "I'm going to drive you up to the mountains."

Nando drove us up the winding roads to the Angeles National Forest in his battered VW Bug. My grandfather said that a city was a reflection of the minds of men and women but that nature was a reflection of the mind of God. I didn't know what that meant until I stepped from Nando's car, dry pinecones crackling under my feet, soft pine needles brushing against each other in whispers of welcome.

I stepped to the edge of the mountain and gasped as I looked up at layer upon layer of stars. I felt the immensity of God, and the last bit of my anger drained from me.

We sat for hours under that black dome of space, ready to fall off the world into the arms of God. I thought about Pocho and the gang, and I knew all that was behind me now. I'd never forget any of it, but I'd never be it again.

I gathered pinecones and pine needles before we left so I could take the fragrance home.

That night the winds blew, rumbling against my window. A branch broke free from the apple tree and hit the glass. I got out of bed, shivering in the cool room that smelled of fresh air and pine needles.

Ana was at my window, wearing a long, flowing white gown like the ones we had drawn in the sand with sticks. The lace train swept behind her, ruffled by the wind, flapping to the edge of the yard.

Ana smiled at me, but it was a sad smile. She held up a baby for me to see. I pressed my palms against the glass, hating this barrier between us. I opened the window, and as I did, Ana's form faded into the thick shadows at the base of the avocado tree.

But a gentle breeze caressed my cheek, and somehow Ana was there, her breath a whisper in my ear telling me to dance. Vamos a bailar.

I stood in the moonlight, and my feet started to move, slow and unsure at first. Then I heard music. At first I thought it was my imagination or maybe that Ana had brought it with her from heaven, but then I realized it was coming from a neighbor's home far away. I stopped and listened to the beat, not bold like the music I was used to, but my feet started to move anyway, trying to find the rhythm.

I danced for a long time, the moon like a halo around me, and finally I could feel Ana beside me again. For only a moment I was with her in heaven, our feet reaching back, urging waves across the ocean.

Then Ana pulled away from me, her hands lingering on my face, then pushing me gently back to earth. The moon set and the darkness surrounded me, but still I danced, finding my place in this new music, waiting for the first rays of dawn to bathe me in a new light.

Lynne Ewing writes extensively for magazines, television, and film. Her first book for young adults, *Drive-By*, was an American Library Association Quick Pick and a New York Public Library Book for the Teen Age.

Ms. Ewing graduated from high school in Lima, Peru, and attended the University of California at Santa Barbara. She spent several years working for the Los Angeles County Department of Public Social Services as a bilingual employee before turning to writing as a full-time career.

SHABANU
by Suzanne Fisher Staples

Life is both sweet and cruel to strong-willed young Shabanu, whose home is the windswept Cholistan Desert of Pakistan. The second daughter in a family with no sons, she's been allowed freedoms forbidden to most Muslim girls. Yet her parents soon grow justifiably concerned that her independence and disinterest in "women's work" will lead to trouble.

As tradition dictates, Shabanu's father has arranged for her to be married in the coming year. Though this will mean an end to her liberty, Shabanu accepts it as her duty to her family. Then a tragic encounter with a wealthy and powerful landowner ruins the marriage plans of her older sister, and it is Shabanu who is called upon to sacrifice everything she's dreamed of. Should she do what is necessary to uphold her family's honor—or should she listen to the stirrings of her own heart?

A Newbery Honor Book
An ALA Best Book for Young Adults
A New York Times Notable Book of the Year
An IRA–CBC Young Adults' Choice

WISE CHILD
by Monica Furlong

In a remote Scottish village, a girl called Wise Child is abandoned by her parents and taken in by Juniper, a sorceress. Under Juniper's kind but stern tutelage, Wise Child thrives. She learns reading, herbal lore, and even the beginnings of magic. Then Wise Child's natural mother—the "black" witch Maeve—reappears, offering the girl a life of ease and luxury. Forced to choose between Maeve and Juniper, Wise Child comes to discover both her true loyalties and her growing supernatural powers. By this time, though, Maeve's evil magic, a mysterious plague, and the fears of superstitious villagers have combined to place Wise Child and Juniper in what may be inescapable danger....

"Mesmerizing and suspenseful." —*New York Newsday*

"Rich in detail, high in excitement, and filled with unforgettable characters." —*Booklist*

An ALA Notable Book
An IRA–CBC Young Adults' Choice

SONGS OF FAITH
by Angela Johnson

Some people stay and some people go. That's just the way it is. The year 1976 is just a few months away, and everyone in town is gearing up for the Bicentennial. But Doreen doesn't feel much like celebrating. It just doesn't seem right, so soon after the Vietnam War. So soon after Mama Dot and Daddy's divorce. So soon after her little brother, Bobo, suddenly stopped talking. Doreen knows for sure this will be a sad summer, an everybody-leaving-me summer.

But under the falling maple leaves, in her mother's embrace, Doreen begins to learn the knowledge of the heart: you're never alone if you have love—and your own song of faith.

♦ "An eloquent and life-affirming novel."
—*Kirkus Reviews* (pointer review)

★ "Heart-wrenching lyricism and fascinating characters....Another tender, eloquent book from a gifted writer." —*Booklist* (starred review)

AVAILABLE FROM DELL LAUREL-LEAF BOOKS

GONE FROM HOME
by Angela Johnson

Meet Sweetness, who has saved an abandoned baby and held up a convenience store, both on the same day. And Starr, who arrives on her Day-Glo orange bicycle to baby-sit for a summer—and changes a family forever. And Victor, who cannot hear, but sees clearly that his brother and sister will soon learn to fly.

In twelve taut, emotional stories, Angela Johnson explores the hardship, hope, and surprising acts of compassion in the lives of young people gone from home.

★ "A remarkable collection."
—*The Horn Book Magazine*, Starred

★ "A beautiful collection of twelve 'short takes' in spare but sparkling prose."
—*School Library Journal*, Starred

★ "In these brief, emotion-packed dramas . . .
the characters, whatever their personal hardships, find shelter in their connection to others, grace in their appreciation of life's uplifting moments."
—*Publishers Weekly*, Starred

WRESTLING STURBRIDGE
by Rich Wallace

Here's the deal. I'm stuck in Sturbridge, Pennsylvania, where civic pride revolves around the high school wrestling team, and the future is as bright as the inside of the cinder block factory where our dads work. And where their dads worked. And where I won't ever work. Not if I can help it.

I'm the second-best 135-pound wrestler in school, behind Al—the first-best 135-pound wrestler in the state. But I want to be state champion as badly as he does, maybe even more. I just haven't figured out how to do it.

I tell myself that I will find the way. I think my whole life depends on it.

★ "A real winner." —*Publishers Weekly* (starred review)

★ "An excellent, understated first novel…Like Ben, whose voice is so strong and clear here, Wallace weighs his words carefully, making every one count."
—*Booklist* (starred review)

An ALA Top Ten Best Book for Young Adults
An ALA Quick Pick for Young Adults

SWALLOWING STONES
by Joyce McDonald

It begins with a free and joyful act—but from then on, Michael finds it impossible even to remember what it felt like to be free and joyful. When he fires his new rifle into the air on his seventeenth birthday, he never imagines that the bullet will end up killing someone. But a mile away, a man *is* killed by that bullet as he innocently repairs his roof. And Michael keeps desperately silent while he watches his world crumble.

Meanwhile, Jenna, the dead man's daughter, copes with a desperation of her own. Through her grief, she tries to understand why she no longer feels comfortable with her boyfriend and why a near stranger named Michael keeps appearing in her dreams.

Suspenseful and powerfully moving, this is the unforgettable story of an accidental crime and its haunting web of repercussions.

"Mesmerizing."
—*School Library Journal*

"Readers will quickly become absorbed in this electrifying portrayal of fear and deception."
—*Publishers Weekly*

An ALA Best Book for Young Adults
A New York Public Library Book for the Teen Age